SUN & DREAM

The Channeler Trilogy Book Two

J. Steven Lamperti

ISBN-13 : 978-1734597486

Lamprey Publishing
LampreyPublishing@gmail.com

Cover Design by James, GoOnWrite.com

Map by Johnny Quan

Printed in the United States of America

The Channeler Trilogy

Moon & Shadow

Sun & Dream

Death & Dragon

The Tales of Liamec

The Wolf's Tooth

By the Sea

Twilight's Fall

The Channeler Trilogy

Sunshine over Hero

The Pirates of Meara

Endymion and the Fae

Dedicated to the one I love,
and hopefully,
loved by the one I dedicate it to.

AUTHOR'S NOTE

Sun & Dream is the second book in the Channeler Trilogy, and it continues the story begun in *Moon & Shadow*. It is written with the expectation that the first book has already been read—stories like this tend to wander, but not backward.

This volume does not stand alone. Its story is intentionally unresolved, and it leads directly into the concluding book, *Death & Dragon*. If you prefer tidy endings, consider keeping that book close at hand; patience will be rewarded.

A brief recap follows for orientation. It is not meant to replace reading Moon & Shadow, but to remind you how Anise arrived here, and why the road ahead is less straightforward than it once seemed.

RECAP

Anise is a young girl who has the potential to be a channeler. Channeling is a form of magic where one conjures spirits or daemons in one's dreams and requests or instructs them in ways they can help one in the real world.

Anise's village was destroyed, and her parents were killed by a nightmare, a creature conjured from dreams by a channeler named Lorenzo. After she and her Aunt Rose fled to a neighboring village, they encountered a young farmer. The farmer, Sebastian, had been going through some strange things. Soon, through events that seemed out of his control, he became the Knight of Moon & Shadow and set off on a quest to defeat Lorenzo and his conjured nightmares. Sebastian triumphed and then used his mysterious powers to reform Lorenzo and set him on the right path.

Our story picks up a few years after the action in *Moon & Shadow* when Anise and her Aunt Rose are feeling settled in the village of Hero.

PROLOGUE

Nestled in the foothills of the Etenies mountains, in the northwest corner of the kingdom of Liamec, was a lake. A pretty little body of water, the lake was a beautiful crystal blue. Cold, it was fed by streams flowing from the mountains to the west. It was high enough in elevation that many of the trees on the lake's western shores were evergreens. The outlet from the lake was a stream that wound east down toward the lower lands. Eventually, this stream gathered force until it joined the Dragon river from the south. Together, they roared into the ocean far to the north and east.

Deer, bears, and wolves came from higher hills and drank the crystal waters. There were smaller creatures living in the woods also. All manner of birds flew through the skies and sang among the trees. Hares and badgers scurried through the underbrush. There were rumors and stories of larger, darker creatures coming down from the mountains.

On the lake's eastern shore was a small, undistinguished town called Lakeside. Lakeside was so small and undistinguished that it's hardly worth mentioning, so we'll leave it in peace for now.

On the western side of the lake, among the evergreens, was the town of Ashton. Ashton was supposedly so named because it had been burned to ash by a dragon's flames and then rebuilt in the distant past. No one in living memory had seen a dragon, and there were other theories as to why the town was named that. One of the industries in Ashton was the production of soap.

Ashton had other distinguishing features. In addition to contributing to the cleanliness of Liamec by producing soap, Ashton made magic, and people trained in magic. In and around Ashton were buildings, places, and people that, put together, constituted an academy of learning. A place where people from all over Liamec, and sometimes further abroad, came to learn how to control and direct forces that allowed the manipulation of reality.

The Academy, as it was referred to throughout Liamec, was housed in a walled enclave adjacent to Ashton. There was also an island in the lake. This island, a short distance through lake waters from the Academy, was known as the Isle of the Wise. The Isle was only accessible to students and faculty of the Academy. Stories and rumors about what was on the Isle were rife among the non-magical citizens of Ashton.

But that's not where our story begins. Our story begins in the village of Hero, in the opposite corner of the kingdom of Liamec.

HERO

1

Anise did not particularly enjoy feeding Uncle Sebastian and Aunt Isabel's chickens. Aunt Isabel had a certain specific way she wanted the feeding done. It wasn't enough to scatter some feed on the ground and let the chickens fend for themselves. The worry was that some greedy ones would take all the food, and others would starve. Isabel said it had happened before. So, she was supposed to put the food in the feeders located around the chicken coop run. Also, she was supposed to feed them in waves. First, put down some food for some, wait a while, and afterward, put down food for the rest.

Anise felt it was a lot of work for some dumb chickens. She knew they were dumb because she'd been playing a game to keep herself amused while feeding them. The game was fun, but it didn't work as well as it should have because the chickens were so stupid.

The game worked as follows: first, she would think of something that she wanted a specific chicken to do. Then, after imagining what she wanted the chicken to do, she would daydream about the chicken doing it and see what happened. For example, she had this one hen that she had been trying to get to fly up on top of the coop. It was a bit hard because while she was daydreaming about getting the chicken to do what she wanted, it was hard to keep feeding them. The first time she tried to do her daydreaming, she started to really fall asleep and only woke up when she felt herself falling down.

After she stirred herself from her daydream, she was excited to see that chicken start to flap its wings and actually take off and fly in the direction of the coop's roof. Unfortunately, at that point, it just flopped around a bit, looked confused, and then landed. That was when she decided that they were too stupid to exist.

The rooster, who she had named Sure, followed her around. He had become excited when she had imagined something about one of the hens. It seemed he had gotten the wrong idea. He followed Anise around, flapping his wings sometimes and scratching at the ground.

Anise slipped into her daydream again and visualized Sure, sitting quietly in the corner of the chicken run. When she woke herself up, he did wander off and seemed to be leaving her alone. Maybe he wasn't quite as stupid as the rest of the chickens.

Betsy stuck her head over the chicken run fence and gave a loud "Heee Awwwwwwww," her mule bray, that was a combination of a donkey's bray and a horse's whinny. The chickens all scattered. Anise was startled as well.

"You dumb mule," said Anise. "You scared me."

Immediately Anise felt awful. For one thing, she loved Betsy, and for another, that was no way to talk to the noble steed of the Knight of Moon and Shadow.

Betsy had been slowing down a little in the last few years, and she'd never really been that noble anyway. Still, she deserved respect for how she had helped Sebastian. When Anise's uncle had transformed into the Knight of Moon & Shadow and saved the town, Betsy had traveled with him throughout the entire quest.

Anise walked over to the chicken run door and out into the yard. Aunt Isabel had asked her to stop by the house when she was finished feeding the chickens. She had something else she wanted to talk to Anise about.

2

Hero was a small settlement in the southeast corner of the kingdom of Liamec. Some called the quiet little town of Hero a village, though the village's mayor would be sure to correct anyone who said that within his hearing. "It's a town!" he would retort, though he wished he could be saying that it was a city in his heart of hearts.

The main street that led past Hero was marked, as were most of the roads in Liamec, by stone way-markers engraved with the names of nearby towns. Travelers on that road would usually keep going past the side lane that led to the town's gates.

Those on their way to the rest of Liamec to the west, the other towns of the Crossroads to the north and east, or sometimes, rarely, to the southeast and the Poignant Pass, would ignore the stone marker reading, Hero. They had more critical destinations in mind. Perhaps the mighty city of Capitol, with the glorious King's Seat where the kings of Liamec had resided for hundreds of years. Maybe the exotic land of France on the other end of the Poignant Pass or other even more exotic lands beyond it.

Those who walked past the turnoff toward Hero did miss something, however. They missed a scenic little town nestled between the Westhaven River on the west and the distant Blue Mountains on the east. It had a mill house, cobbled streets (mostly), a market square, and a solid wooden town gate.

Hero's claim to fame, and the source of its name, was an event that had happened several years ago. Towns and villages that were part of the loose confederation of communities called the Crossroads were suddenly attacked by creatures out of nightmares. Anise and her Aunt Rose had come to Hero, then called Westhavenfieldbrook, as refugees, fleeing an attack on their town by one of those nightmare monsters.

An unremarkable villager named Sebastian had suddenly acquired extraordinary powers and magical artifacts, which enabled him to defend the village against the attacks. After Sebastian's defense of the town, and his subsequent defeat of the channeler behind the attack, Lorenzo, things returned to normal.

The mayor, sensing an opportunity to grow his village into a city, had renamed the sleepy little town of Westhavenfieldbrook: Hero and built a monument to Sebastian's victory in the town square.

The story of Sebastian's adventures became well known, and songs were written that entertained many people in other parts of Liamec. Unfortunately, this hadn't translated into income or growth for Hero. Life in the peaceful village went on much as before.

3

Anise opened the door of the house that had been her second home for the last few years. Uncle Sebastian and Aunt Isabel weren't really her real aunt and uncle. She didn't have any real family, except for Aunt Rose. But, since Anise and Aunt Rose had moved to Hero, Anise had adopted Sebastian and Isabel as her aunt and uncle. She spent almost as much time at their house as at the bakery with Aunt Rose. Of course, Anise slept at the bakery. Sometimes she still missed her parents. Sometimes she cried quietly in bed at night. But not as often as she used to.

Sebastian's house's white-washed wattle and daub exterior still looked the same. But, since Isabel had been living there, the interior had been redecorated with a woman's touch. Linen curtains waved in the gentle breeze coming in through the open shutters, and there were throw cushions on the wooden bench against one wall. The seat had been lovingly crafted by Isabel's mother, the town carpenter.

In a throwback to Sebastian's bachelor past, his father's sword still hung in its place of honor over the mantle. Above the blade, in the spot where Anise felt it should be, was an image of the moon. To honor the Knight of Moon & Shadow, who he called the "Hero of Hero," The Mayor had had a portrait painted of the moon for Sebastian. The full moon shone down on a fence running through a cow pasture in the picture. There was a face on the moon in the painting. The face was partially the artist's idea of the Man in the Moon. And, partially, it was his interpretation of Sebastian's description of his encounters with the lunar spirit.

Anise once told Sebastian that she didn't think it was an accurate likeness of Luna. He had just given her an odd look as if he was surprised she was familiar with Luna's appearance.

Even though it didn't really look like Luna, Anise sometimes felt the portrait was trying to talk to her.

Anise looked around the room. She didn't see Isabel, but in the corner was Twi's crib. She started. Twi stood in the corner of his crib, staring fiercely at her. He looked intense, not making a sound, just focused on what she would do next. Twi's crib was a little unusual in that Sebastian had installed slats across the top to match those on the sides. He had been capable of climbing out of his crib for months.

Anise laughed. She shook her finger at him.

"You don't even know that you're a baby, do you," she said indulgently.

Twi was Sebastian and Isabel's son. Anise thought of him as her brother. She had, she felt, helped raise him. He was only a bit over one and a half, but he sometimes acted like an old man. "An old soul," Lilith said. His full name was Twilight, but they all called him Twi for short.

Anise was often given the job of watching Twi. She complained to Sebastian, Isabel, and anyone else who would listen that he was a trial to watch as he tried to escape any chance he got.

"I have no idea where he thinks he's going to go," she grumbled.

Anise had a theory. She had heard how the wee folk sometimes snuck into people's houses and swapped babies. A changeling, they called the baby that they left. She told Sebastian this once.

He just smiled at her. "He has my hair and his mother's eyes," he said. "I don't think we can blame anyone other than ourselves for him."

After Sebastian said that, Anise inspected Twi's and Isabel's eyes. Blue-green: a perfect match. The color made her think of how she imagined the sea looked. There were rumors that Isabel's father, Isiah Fisher, had come to Hero from somewhere near the sea.

Anise had asked Lilith about changelings as well. Lilith

14

was the village's cunning woman. She knew about things that other people didn't. Her answer had been less reassuring than Sebastian's. She had said, "Oh, probably not. The wee folk don't do that so much anymore."

Anise stepped a little further into the room. "Aunt Isabel?"

4

Aunt Isabel had given Anise the job of watching Twilight. She and Uncle Sebastian had somewhere that they needed to be that evening. Aunt Rose had told her something similar. The coincidence made Anise suspicious, but she didn't mind, as she had nothing else to do. Her friend Mary had to cover for her sister, Anne, who had skipped out on her turn to work at the mayor's office. So, Anise would have been at home anyway.

Mary and Anne were the miller's daughters. Mary was Anise's best friend. They shared an interest in things like reading that most of the rest of the villagers didn't have time for. Anne, Mary's older sister, had become boy obsessed and was always sneaking off to meet someone.

Twilight was quiet in his crib for the moment, so Anise used the time to try to solve a wooden puzzle that Isabel's mother had made for her. It was a little wooden bird in a cage. It was cleverly carved and put together so you could work the bird between the bars if you knew the trick or sometimes if you just fiddled with it enough. She had managed to get the bird out of the cage and was trying to put it back.

Anise looked up from the puzzle. The quiet in the room made her suspicious. Twilight was sometimes calm, but not usually for very long or without some reason. She looked over at the crib.

The baby was crouched in the corner of the crib, with his back turned toward her. His body was moving rhythmically back and forth. A low rasping sound that she hadn't noticed came to her attention.

Anise stood as quietly as she could and walked over to the crib to see what he was doing.

She gasped. Twilight had gotten hold of one of the table knives, and he was using it to cut at one of the slats on the crib.

"You monster," she cried and reached through the slats to grab the knife from him. There was a little pile of sawdust on the floor beneath the slat.

She put the knife on the table, unfastened the latch on the top of the crib, and swung it open. Reaching into the crib, she grabbed Twi, lifted him out, and pressed him to her body. She squeezed him against herself hard, trying to determine the exact amount of pressure necessary to compress all the rebellion out of him.

Twilight grunted. He met her eyes with his own, reached out, and grabbed her nose, his thumb inside her nostril and the other fingers gripping firmly.

Anise loosened her grip, her eyes tearing, and reached one hand up to the little baby's hand on her nose, trying to free herself. She put him on the floor, blinked tears from her eyes, and said, "All right, you want some attention?"

The baby stood, balancing precariously on his little feet. He smiled at her as he swayed back and forth.

There was a game that Sebastian played with his son. They both loved it, and it was one of the few tricks that calmed Twilight down when he got overwrought. Sebastian had crafted two little swords out of wood, so small as to be more like knives than swords, and he and his son would have little duels. Anise used this sometimes to calm the baby.

She got the sticks and gave the baby his. She laughed when he took it and turned his body to the side to present a smaller target to his opponent. He almost tumbled backward and barely kept his footing.

Sebastian had asked his mother-in-law if she could craft improved swords for the game, but she turned the job down. As the town carpenter, Mrs. Fisher was very skilled with wood, but she responded as a grandmother.

"You can't teach a baby to sword fight," she said, "it doesn't make any sense. And, anyway, you shouldn't be doing that. That's how you lose an eye!"

Sebastian had insisted that his father had taught him at that age. "'Sooner learned, never burned,' my father always used to say."

"He always did have the strangest sayings," said Mrs. Fisher. She shook her head. "No one around here says anything like that."

After an hour of vigorous battle, Anise finally got Twi to bed.

5

They were all sitting on the bench in a row. Uncle Sebastian, Aunt Isabel, Aunt Rose, and Lilith. The other side of the table was free. They were all looking at her, obviously expecting her to sit down opposite them.

What have I done wrong now? Anise thought.

It was the dining room table at one end of the main room of Isabel and Sebastian's house. Twilight was on his feet in his crib at the far end of the room. He was holding onto the slats with both hands. His face showed that he was astonished that he wasn't sitting at the table with his parents.

Anise trudged haltingly toward the table. She gazed down at the tabletop to avoid meeting the adult's eyes.

It must have been something terrible, she thought. *They all look so stern.*

The surface of the table wasn't a bad distraction. Isabel's mother, grandma Fisher, had made the table as a wedding present for Sebastian and Isabel. She had spent months working on it in secret. The tabletop was a miracle of inlaid wood. The patterns and shapes in the inlay were seemingly random but made you feel like they weren't. Anise had spent quite a bit of time admiring it.

"Have a seat, Anise," said Sebastian. He didn't sound angry, more worried.

Anise sat down. After studying the tabletop for another moment, she glanced up. Isabel was smiling at her, Rose was looking down, Lilith looked grim, and Sebastian met her gaze with an earnest expression.

Rose glanced up. Her eyes were a bit red as if she had been crying. Anise was sure that couldn't be it. She had never seen Rose cry.

"Anise, dear," she started.

"What's this about?" said Anise, "What did I do wrong?"

Lilith leaned forward. She put her arms in front of her on the table and met Anise's gaze. Being among friends, Lilith wasn't wearing her hood or trying to put on her village cunning woman act. She wasn't trying to put on a show like she sometimes did, but she had gained a certain gravitas in the last few years. The touch of gray in her hair at the temples didn't hurt either.

"Anise," she said, "when a young woman gets to be a certain age, changes start to happen in her body..."

"This isn't going to be about the birds and the bees, is it?" said Anise. "I know all about that from school. Mrs. Shoemaker won't let us talk about it during school hours, but the kids talk at recess."

Lilith leaned back, defeated.

"Anise," said Sebastian, "in the foothills of the Etenies mountains is a lake, and on that lake's shores is an academy—"

"I know all about the Academy. Lilith told me," said Anise. "Why are you all here? What did I do wrong?"

Sebastian turned and exchanged a glance with Isabel.

Isabel ventured. "Anise, dear," she said, "if you'd let anyone finish, we're trying to talk to you about something."

Rose started crying.

Anise stared; Rose never cried. Something was really wrong.

6

Sebastian tried again. "Anise," he said, "we're trying to tell you, without much luck so far, that we've talked about it, and we think that it's time for an important and necessary change in your life."

Rose started crying harder.

Sebastian looked grim. "It doesn't have to be a bad thing. That Academy I mentioned? Lilith says you need to be trained there."

It became clear to Anise why Rose was crying. Lilith had hinted at this to Anise before, but she hadn't taken it seriously. She scanned the faces across the table. Rose wouldn't meet her eyes. Isabel was smiling with what was clearly supposed to be an encouraging smile. It was clear that Lilith wanted to say something.

"Do I have to go?" Anise said. A little knot of nerves started to form in her stomach. Her voice broke, and she felt she should have waited to speak.

"There was some resistance," said Sebastian, glancing sympathetically at Rose, "but I'll let Lilith address that question."

Lilith was eager to speak. She met Anise's gaze directly and firmly. "That's why I mentioned your age, Anise. The beginning of adulthood corresponds with the onset of the full powers of magic. We've talked before about your potential, and I've given you what training I can, but you have a great deal of power in you, and I'm not equipped to help you bring it out fully."

Anise shook her head. "I don't need to know magic," she said, "I'll stay here, and those stupid people at that academy can do their magic without me."

Lilith shook her head as well. "I'm sorry, Anise, it

doesn't work like that." She looked thoughtful and smoothed a lock of brown hair with a streak of gray out of her face. She continued, "If you had less potential for power, or were showing signs of being good at alchemy, maybe, but you're going to be a channeler. Channeling is the wild card of magic. It's hard to control, hard to understand, and hard to use constructively. If you don't learn how to control and understand your abilities, they will be a danger to you, us, and the whole village." She frowned. "The country, possibly. Your uncle, Sebastian, has offered to travel with you." Lilith turned to look at Sebastian.

"It could be fun, Anise," said Sebastian. "It'd be just you and me on an adventure."

"I can't leave," said Anise. "Who would watch Twilight?" She turned and looked over at the baby. He was still watching the meeting intently. It seemed he thought he had something to contribute.

Sebastian smiled at the comment. "I think we can keep an eye on him," he said, "He's just a baby, after all."

"I don't want to go," said Anise. She felt like she was facing an oncoming storm.

"I'm sorry, Anise," said Lilith. "There isn't any choice. Channeling the spirit of a squirrel or even a dryad from a local tree is one thing. But, two years ago, the moon itself took an interest in us and our village."

Anise looked down at the ground. She felt defeated. "Could we take Betsy?" she said.

Sebastian hesitated. "Betsy's getting a little older," he said. "I guess we could ask Mr. Thatcher the farrier if he thinks she'd be up for the trip."

7

The crowd gathered at the main gate to see Anise, Sebastian, and Betsy off, reminded Anise of the Knight of Moon & Shadow's quest. The mayor was there, Isabel, Isabel's mother, and Lilith. Mr. Thatcher, the town farrier, was there. Whenever anyone in the village had a question about animals, especially horses, mules, or donkeys, they would turn to him. He had given Betsy an extensive medical exam, mainly just opening her mouth to look at her teeth. She hadn't liked it and had tried to bite him. He had pronounced her ornery but healthy.

The morning was stressful. It was a long journey, and Anise wasn't going to be able to travel back and forth very often. It wasn't clear how or when she would next be back in the town of Hero. Rose wasn't taking this well. People had been trying to get her to stop crying all morning.

Sebastian would be traveling with Anise, and once he helped her settle, he would be coming back. Still, the Academy was all the way on the other side of Liamec, and he would be gone for a long time. Isabel was not terribly happy about this.

Isabel held Twi on her hip. He was looking around at all the action with enormous interest. Apparently, he was contemplating how he'd manage a departure gathering differently if he were in charge.

The mayor was relieved to see that Mr. Arkwright, the smith, wasn't there. They had had a falling out about a year ago or so. It wasn't about the cobbling of the town streets of Hero. The cobbles that proudly covered the main square now ran all the way down Main Street to this very gate that they were standing beneath. No, Mr. Arkwright had dared to run in the last Mayoral election.

It hadn't been a real challenge. The mayor had won

handily. Still, the notion that one of his own aldermen, someone he had taken under his wing and mentored, would stab him in the back like that had left a bitter taste in his mouth.

"Citizens of Hero," cried the mayor, using his best 'talking to a crowd' voice. "Good morning to you all!" Most of the town was still asleep, but the mayor thought it was best to keep up appearances. "Our Sebastian, Our Hero of Hero, is leaving us on another quest."

Isabel and her mother shared a 'who does he think he's talking to' look.

The mayor turned off the voice, walked over to Sebastian, and clapped him on the shoulder.   "Take good care of our little Alice, my boy," he said.

Perhaps it's a good thing that Anise was just starting her journey to magic, as otherwise, the look she gave the mayor might have made him burst into flame.

Rose approached with a bundle of pastries wrapped in wax paper in her hand. She had stopped crying for the moment, but her eyes were lined in red. She handed the bundle to Anise. They had already loaded the mule with supplies. *These must be something extra*, thought Anise.

"They're for Sebastian. Raisin cakes. He loves them," Rose whispered.

Rose started crying quietly again. She reached out, gathered Anise to herself, and hugged her tightly. "You be careful out there," she said. "Listen to your uncle. Don't talk to strangers. Be strong and proud."

Isabel ran forward. Awkwardly, because holding Twilight offset her balance, she put one hand on Sebastian's chest and stood on tip-toes to kiss him. The morning sunlight cast her shadow across the ground behind her. The black ring on one of her fingers seemed like it absorbed rather than reflected the light. Sebastian grabbed her around the waist, pulled both her and the baby into himself, and returned the kiss.

8

Once they were out of sight of Hero and Rose's tears, Anise felt a little better. The sun was shining, she was walking beside her uncle and her favorite mule, and they were on an adventure. Betsy was getting excited too. She announced it to the morning and the world with a big, "Heee awwwwwwww!"

They turned left at the intersection on the edge of town. The leftward way led west, away from the Blue Mountains and toward the heart of the kingdom of Liamec. They crossed the old stone bridge over the Westhaven River. The wide road led on as far as they could see to the west. It was cleared for ten feet on each side for visibility and safety. Now that they had left Hero's fields behind, there were untended forests on the roadsides.

Anise ran ahead down the dusty lane, turned toward her uncle and Betsy, raised her arms up like a bird, and charged back towards them as if she were flying. Betsy flicked her ears disdainfully.

"Isn't it a beautiful day, Uncle?" she said breathlessly.

"It is, Anise," said Sebastian. "Though that morning sunshine you are enjoying will feel less friendly in a few hours when it gets hot."

It was late summer, about the hottest time of year. They were hoping to reach the Academy in time for the start of the fall session.

Anise fell into step beside her uncle. She looked up at the blue sky, the few clouds, and the bright morning sun. She looked thoughtful. "Does the sun have a spirit, like Luna and the moon?"

"Of course," said Sebastian. "Helios is the god of the sun. He's up there right now, looking down on us. They say he sees everything. If you look at the sun directly and squint the right way, you can see his face, just like you can see the face of Luna in the full moon."

Anise turned obediently and started to look at the bright morning sun.

Sebastian put his hand between her eyes and the blazing orb with a laugh. "I was kidding, Anise," he said. "You shouldn't look directly at the sun. It's bad for your eyes."

9

Anise ran through a dark wood. The branches of the trees grabbed at her clothing. Moonlight filtered through the trees, barely, just enough for her to see the narrow trail by the faint glimmer. Her heartbeat was a drum roll through her chest.

Where's Aunt Rose? she thought. *I just need to make it to a clearing, and I'll find her.*

The next howl was closer.

They're catching up with me, Anise thought.

In her mind's eye, she could see the face of one of the wolves chasing her. The wolf was panting, her tongue hanging out of her mouth. Her eyes looked fierce, but they also looked fearful.

They're not just angry—they're scared, thought Anise. *They're scared because they're angry, which makes them more scared.*

Where's Aunt Rose? she thought again. *If I can only find Aunt Rose, I'll be all right.*

There were rustling sounds and the sound of bodies rushing throughout the underbrush around her. Somehow she was running fast enough to keep ahead of the wolves.

They're scared because I am, she thought.

"Anise," said Sebastian urgently in an anxious whisper. "You need to wake up now." He shook her shoulder as she lay tightly curled up in her bedroll.

Anise opened her eyes. Her uncle stood over her. He was fully dressed in the outfit that Isabel had prepared for him for the journey. Anise had helped her. The white dyed thick linen britches were intended for protection, but they had spent more thought on the jerkin. It was double-layered durable cloth, with stitching quilting the fabric into compartments. Anise had had the inspiration to stuff the quilted pockets with thistledown. It had taken her a long time to gather enough from the fields around Hero.

Isabel dyed the padded jerkin purple and Sebastian's leather boots black. The intent was to give him the look of the Knight of Moon and Shadow. Sebastian was a little unsure when he saw it, but he wore it for Isabel.

Anise looked around. The campfire was still burning, though it had burned a little low, and the firewood was in short supply. The fire illuminated the circle of large boulders that stood around the spot they had picked to camp. Betsy stood over on the other side of the campsite, nickering fearfully. Her lead was lashed to a tree. Otherwise, she might have bolted.

"There's something out there. I think it's wolves," said Sebastian. He was holding his sword in his hand. "I need you awake in case we have to run."

A howl cut through the night air.

10

Anise stood. She looked groggy to Sebastian. He saw her make an effort to pull herself together. "It's all right, Uncle," she said. "They don't want to be here any more than we want them here. They're just here because of my dream."

"Anise," said Sebastian, "this is serious. The fire is keeping them at bay for the moment, but we're running out of firewood."

"Just a minute," said Anise. "I'll get rid of them." She raised one hand, palm outward, toward Sebastian. She shut her eyes, her breathing slowed, and she swayed back and forth.

Sebastian gazed at her. *Had she fallen back asleep, standing up?* He resisted the impulse to shake her again and looked around the campsite. It had seemed a safe spot to camp for the evening. What felt like an eternity ago. The circle of large boulders sheltered them from the wind. There was already a circle of smaller stones forming a firepit where numerous previous travelers had made fires. There was a place to tie up Betsy close, but not so close that she would be putting her nose into their dinners.

He re-evaluated the site from a more defensive perspective. There were several spots where there were gaps in the boulders. If the wolves launched a coordinated attack, they would be hard to stop. *They wouldn't do that, would they?*

He held his sword in front of himself as he walked toward one of the gaps.

Anise shuddered and opened her eyes.

"There," she said. "I've told them as best I could. Some of them didn't listen, though."

She looked thoughtful. "They really don't like the fire."

The firelight lit up the circle of standing boulders. With

a loud howl, a wolf burst into the light. The flames and light from the fire's glowing embers reflected off its eyes. It was a gray wolf, not too big, but plenty big enough to be terrifying.

Betsy reared up onto her hind legs. Her forehooves lashed through the air. For a moment, where a tired mule had stood, there was a mighty war stallion. The steed of the Knight of Moon & Shadow. Then Betsy flopped back down, and her forelock fell over her eyes.

With his sword in one hand, trying to hold the beast at bay, Sebastian grabbed a brand from the fire with the other. He moved to stay in between the creature and Anise. The wolf crouched by the edge of the clearing, between two boulders, growling. Sebastian didn't see or hear any others coming.

Sword in one hand, burning brand in the other, Sebastian took a step toward the creature. He had the feeling that Anise was right. The wolf didn't want to be here, especially with the rest of the pack not making an appearance. It snarled, baring its teeth.

Sebastian swung the blazing brand and managed to nick the creature on the top of its back. It yelped, and he saw embers off the flaming wood scatter like sparks around it.

The wolf decided it had had enough. It turned and ran back through the gap between the boulders.

11

The sun was shining brightly in another beautiful sky the following morning. Betsy was ambling along behind Sebastian and Anise. Even though Sebastian walked in front, holding Betsy's lead, she still set the pace. Nobody could hurry Betsy up if she didn't want them to. It didn't seem like the mule was in any rush to get to their destination.

Sebastian turned to Anise and said, "Anise, what did you mean about the wolves being there because of you?"

"It's channeling. Lilith told me about it. Apparently, I have the potential to be a very good channeler," Anise said proudly. She smiled in a way that lit up her face. "Channeling is when you make people, animals, or spirits do things in your dreams. The wolves were coming to get us because that's what was happening in my dream."

Sebastian looked at her sternly. "Anise," he said. "We almost... We almost... We could have died. If I hadn't woken you or the wolves hadn't left, we could have died."

Anise looked a little shamefaced, "That's what Lilith said. I need to go to the Academy for—" She hesitated. "—control. She said they could teach me control. She said that the cunning folk don't do much channeling. They do illusions, elemental magic, and potions, but they don't do channeling."

Sebastian said thoughtfully, "Well, I guess we'll have to keep you happy so that you don't have any more bad dreams until then."

Sebastian stood by the stone way-markers at an intersection. He had pulled the map that Anise and Mary made for the trip out of Betsy's saddlebags. He was glaring at the parchment, the furrow between his brows deep enough to get lost in.

"Anise," he called out, "can you help me with this map?"

Anise came closer and looked over his shoulder. "What's wrong?"

"The town names on these way stones don't match any of the town names on the map." Sebastian waved the parchment in Anise's face.

Anise and her friend Mary had visited the town library in preparation for the trip. They had managed to get a piece of parchment from Brone Tailor, the town scribe.

Anise had always been very impressed with the town library. It was just a modest room in the town hall, but the bookshelf against one side of the room must have had twenty books in it. Anise hadn't thought that there were that many books in the world.

When Brone pulled the map out of a drawer and spread it out on a table, Anise had no idea what they should do. The parchment was covered with pretty little pictures, lines, and dots. There was no way they could make a copy of it.

Brone helped them. They didn't copy the pictures, just the town names of the bigger towns and lines to show roads. They had a spider web of lines connecting dots with labels written on them when they were done.

Anise and Sebastian compared the labels on the map with the names on the stones. At each intersection on the major roads of Liamec, there were stone way-markers. The stone way-markers pointed down roads, listing the name of the closest village and then usually the name of another larger town further off in the same direction. Eventually, they found a label on the map that matched one of the names carved on a stone and continued on their way.

GRISPUT

1

Sebastian and Anise were gathering wood and kindling for the evening fire. Sebastian told Anise that they should collect more than the previous night. "I don't think it'll happen again, but better to be safe than sorry," he said.

He was dumping a load of firewood near the fire pit when he saw someone approaching from the road. Betsy looked up and flicked her ears toward the approaching person.

As Anise drew near from the other direction, Sebastian studied the figure.

It was a young man. He was dressed in rags, dirty, faded britches, and a torn linen tunic. He had a beat-up backpack on his back, a small knife in a sheath belted at his waist, but didn't seem to be carrying anything else. Sebastian assumed the young man was looking for a hand-out from the disheveled clothes and the grime.

Anise reached the fire-pit and dropped the wood and kindling she had found. Sebastian called out, "We don't have much money, but I suppose we could spare a copper." He reached for one of Betsy's saddlebags, looking for his coin purse.

The young man stepped closer. He looked indignant. He stood up straight, met Sebastian's eye, and said, "I am no beggar. I am Briac, the magnificent, world-famous minstrel!"

He opened his backpack and pulled out a battered lute. Holding it in one hand, he executed a smooth minstrel bow, one leg stiff, the other bent, as he leaned forward.

"Uncle!" said Anise. Sebastian wasn't sure what she was reacting to. He didn't feel like his assumption had been unwarranted.

Briac played a few notes on his lute. He again bowed

toward Anise, "At your service, my lady," he said. Anise giggled and glanced down at the ground. He nodded toward Sebastian. "And you, sir."

Sebastian noticed that the lute was missing a string. Briac still managed to make a pleasant sound with it. He was young, just a few years older than Anise. Through the dirt, he looked healthy and fit. Sebastian started to regret his unwelcoming behavior.

"Briac," he said, "as a fellow traveler, would you care to join us at our campsite this evening?"

Briac smiled. "I would be honored," he said. He reached once again into his backpack and pulled out a withered turnip. "I will, of course, contribute," he said, flourishing the vegetable. "For the soup."

2

Sebastian hadn't planned on making a traveler's stew that evening, but he changed the menu to include Briac's turnip. Rose, Isabel, and Mrs. Fisher had packed them food and supplies that should last a long time. Still, they didn't know how long the journey would take, so he was careful to first use the more perishable things.

Sebastian made a point of adding the turnip to the stew at a moment when Briac was looking, so he knew his offering was accepted. As they gathered around the campfire, Sebastian studied the young man. At one point, as he walked past, Sebastian detected an unpleasant smell. Given the state of his clothing, that wasn't surprising.

Sebastian noticed that what he thought was dirt on the young man's face was a trace of hair on his upper lip. Either he was trying to grow a mustache, or shaving was also not part of his hygiene regime. His hair might be a light shade of brown after a bath.

His tunic was ripped down the front. A few chest hairs showed through the rip. Sebastian thought it seemed like the first shoots of new growth from a garden. He caught Anise looking at Briac admiringly.

"Isn't he pretty?" she whispered to Sebastian when Briac was on the other side of the campfire.

Pretty smelly, thought Sebastian, but he didn't say anything.

After they got bowls of stew and sat, Briac announced, "I just played for the gentry and mayor of the town of Hero. They loved my new song."

Sebastian sat up. "We just came from Hero," he said.

"Oh, did I say Hero?" said Briac. "I meant Hercule. A different town."

"You write songs?" said Anise. "Can you play us one?"

"Of course," said Briac. "What minstrel doesn't play for his supper?" He stood and took another bow in her direction. "As soon as we are done with our stew, I will play you my new song, the *Lay of the Knight of Moon & Shadow*."

The young man looked at Anise and Sebastian inquiringly. "You know the story, of course? The tale of how the small-town farmer was summoned by Luna, the lunar spirit, to save his village?" Then he smiled. "Of course you do. You said you just came from Hero."

Anise shot a glance at Sebastian.

Briac continued, "The *Ballad of the Hero* felt too long to me. *The Man Who Pulled the Moon From the Sky* has a boring melody. I think I've improved on them both."

3

The flickering firelight cast a warm glow over the evening as the three sat around the campsite. The meal was over, and Briac pulled his lute out of his battered backpack. He played a little introductory riff and then began to sing.

A hero born of night and dream,
From farmer's field, across hill and stream.
The wind, the moon, the dark, his might,
He saves the world through moonlit night.

A night, oh Knight, a night so dark,
Stop evil dreams to take their mark,
Lo, moon & shadow will not fall,
A knight, oh knight, please heed our call.

The hero rises when nightmares come,
The moon his strength. Her will be done.
His father's sword, his good right arm,
his heart so true, shields all from harm.

A night, oh Knight, a night so dark,
Stop evil dreams to take their mark,
Lo, moon & shadow will not fall,
A knight, oh knight, please heed our call.

And when at last, the nightmares' gone,
struck down by virtue, shadow, and brawn.
Our hero, humbly, fades into night
until he's needed to resume the fight.

A night, oh Knight, a night so dark,
Stop evil dreams to take their mark,
Lo, moon & shadow will not fall,
A knight, oh knight, please heed our call.

There was a moment of silence around the campfire when Briac finished. He strummed the last chord, then paused; Anise released her breath. She sat up straight and clapped her hands. "That was beautiful," she said. She smiled at Briac. He returned the smile.

"Well sung," said Sebastian, "I really admire how you play around that missing string."

Briac laughed and said, "It'll be hard to get used to having it back once I get a new one."

Sebastian threw Briac a water flask. "Here, son, I think singing must be thirsty work." He smiled gently at Briac. "After you've taken a drink, you might want to wash your face. I think you've got a bit of dirt on your lip there."

Anise gave Sebastian a disgusted look. Briac looked hurt.

"It is a lovely song," Sebastian continued thoughtfully. "Did you think about adding more of the story's facts into your lyrics? It's a pretty song, but it doesn't really tell the story, does it?"

Briac scoffed. "Does no one understand abstraction anymore? Everyone knows the story."

Sebastian replied, "If you're writing a song about an event, aren't you usually trying to communicate with the people that don't know the story?"

Anise interjected, "I think you should keep your eyes open when you sing. It will help you connect with your audience."

4

Anise was sitting by the campfire. The moon was shining down on the campsite. She wasn't sure it had been full when she went to sleep, but it was full now. Anise recognized that she was in a dream. She thought she saw Luna, the lunar spirit, wink at her from her position in the sky. Sebastian, Betsy, and Briac were nowhere in sight. Once she knew she was in a dream, she felt in control.

There was a circle of firelight shining on the stones around the campfire. Around and across the fire from her were nine elegant ladies. Anise was more impressed by how elegantly dressed they were than by who they were. They didn't look like they were sitting around a campfire at the side of the road. They could have been dressed for a ball. A little out of fashion, perhaps, but elegant nonetheless.

"So," said Anise in a business-like manner, "you're the muses, right? Who's who?"

One of the ladies swept forward confidently and pronounced, "I am Calliope, the elder sister."

Behind her, there was a chorus of name declarations. Anise could only make out a few.

"Poly."

"Clio."

"Thalia."

Anise sighed wearily. "Who's in charge of music?" she said.

"That's me. I'm Euterpe," one of them said. She wore a laurel wreath on her head, a light red gown, and she met Anise's gaze with a warm smile.

"If I might have a word," said Anise.

Sebastian awoke with a start. He felt a surge of

adrenaline. He reached to his belt for the hilt of his sword and rose to a sitting position. *Where are Betsy's saddlebags? Someone's trying to steal the moon.*

Sebastian looked around the campsite. Anise and Briac were still asleep. The first hint of light was just showing in the eastern sky. He wasn't even wearing his sword. There was no one there but them.

Before Anise opened her eyes, the strains of distant music reached her ears. It was pretty, exotic sounding. She recognized the sounds of Briac's lute, but the tune was unfamiliar.

She smelled something as well. She opened her eyes and saw Sebastian bustling around the embers of the fire. He was melting some cheese onto slices of rye bread on a flat rock near the warm coals.

Sebastian saw her open her eyes. "I know we're not supposed to break our fast until midday," he said, "but I thought a bit of bread would give us strength for walking today."

Anise looked around for Briac. She didn't see him, and the sounds of his lute were a bit distant.

Sebastian noticed her look and said, "He didn't want to wake you. He said something about musical inspiration. I think he's not far. It sounds pretty, doesn't it?"

5

After eating, Sebastian started getting Betsy ready for the day's travels. She grumbled, as she always did when he put on her saddlebags. At one point, she tried to nip his hand. "What kind of gratitude is that for finding us this lovely campsite?" said Sebastian.

When they made their way over to the roadway, Briac seemed in no hurry to leave. Sebastian turned to him and said, "Which way are you going, son?"

Briac pointed down the road in the same direction they were heading.

Sebastian, somewhat reluctantly, said, "Well, I guess we'll be traveling together, at least for a little." Anise smiled.

Briac put his hand on the hilt of his dagger and said, "There's safety in numbers."

Sebastian walked a bit ahead. Anise held Betsy's lead, and Briac walked beside her.

"This is Betsy," said Anise. "Betsy, meet Briac." Briac started to reach out to touch Betsy's nose. "Careful," continued Anise. "If she's not in a good mood, she might try to bite you."

Betsy assessed Briac's hand skeptically. She flicked one ear forward and the other back. She might have spun one of them around in a circle if she could. It took her a while to get used to new people.

"Betsy," said Briac thoughtfully. "You named her after the mule in *The Man Who Pulled the Moon From the Sky*." He looked again at the gray hair around her muzzle and continued, "Or, renamed her." Anise laughed.

"I had a dream last night," said Briac to Anise.

"Uh-huh," said Anise, looking at him.

"There was a woman in my dream. She encouraged me with my music. That tune I was playing this morning felt like it came from that dream." He looked bemused.

Sebastian went to the way-stones at the next intersection and pulled out his map to check the names. Briac came over and looked over his shoulder. "What kind of map is that?" he complained. "There aren't any pictures or colors. Shouldn't it have the emblems for the towns or the flag colors of the houses on it?"

"That would be nice," said Sebastian. "But this is all we have. You've traveled quite a bit. Maybe you can help me."

Briac scoffed. "Not with that map." He walked back to where Anise and Betsy were standing. It occurred to Sebastian that it was likely that Briac couldn't read. Hero was an unusual town in that it had a schoolhouse, and all the town's children got a school education.

Sebastian thought that maybe Briac would split off and go a different direction at the intersection. He seemed content to continue traveling the same way they were.

6

An arrow came arching through the air. It hit the hard-packed earth of the road right in front of Sebastian and skittered off to one side. He stopped walking forward immediately. "Hestia's hips!" came a voice from the woods off to one side of the roadway.

"Stand and deliver!" a deeper voice called out.

"We're standing, we're standing," said Sebastian quickly. He stepped back to be just a little in front of his traveling companions.

Five men stepped out from the tree line, though there might have been more hiding in the underbrush. Two of them stayed back in the trees, bows trained on the travelers. The other three walked forward to the edge of the roadway.

As they walked forward, Sebastian took stock of Briac and Anise. Anise seemed calm. She was still young enough to assume that her uncle would take care of her. Briac had his hand on the hilt of his dagger. He was watching the oncoming men very intently. Sebastian met the young man's eyes, moved his own hand toward his belt, and shook his head. Briac moved his hand away from the hilt. *He's not a coward*, Sebastian thought.

The men reached the travelers. They were roughly dressed: worn leather clothes, well-traveled but patched and maintained. The one in the middle, probably the one who had called out, was one of the largest men Sebastian had ever seen. He looked more like a bear than a man between his size and the thick brown hair that mostly covered his face.

The man to his right said apologetically, "The arrow was supposed to hit the ground and stick there, quivering. It would have been more dramatic."

Briac stepped forward next to Sebastian and said, "I am

Briac, the splendid, and these are my traveling companions. They are under my protection."

The bear-man ignored Briac and casually said to Sebastian, "Are you rich, or do you work for the prince regent?"

"I can honestly say no to both," said Sebastian.

The big man looked disappointed. The third man, who hadn't spoken yet, said, "Well, can't we take their money anyway?"

The second man, who had mentioned the arrow, went to retrieve it. The big man turned to the third one. "You remember what the Raven said. The rich and powerful, not the common folk."

Sebastian held back a start when the bear-like man mentioned the Raven. He'd heard of the Raven. The outlaw band called the Raven's men was getting a bit of a reputation in these parts.

The big man turned back toward Sebastian, a momentary hopeful gleam reappearing in his eyes.

"You aren't by any chance a tax collector, are you?"

"Sorry," said Sebastian.

The big man looked disappointed again but resigned. He waved to his companions, and they started back towards the woods. He turned again to Sebastian and said, "You folk be about your way. Be careful out there. The roads can be dangerous." He and his companions all disappeared into the shadows under the trees with that final word.

7

A nise dropped behind Sebastian, Briac, and Betsy. Sebastian and Briac were discussing sharpening blades as they walked down the road. Sebastian was very insistent that it was essential to sharpen your blade frequently. Briac argued that excessive sharpening of an edge that wasn't used was unnecessary and could wear it out. Anise found the topic excruciatingly dull.

She heard a rustling in the underbrush just behind her. She turned, a little wary after their encounter with the outlaws.

A family of quail burst from underneath a bush and started across the trail. It was a mother quail followed by her brood. The mother looked from side to side as she led the babies onward. The baby birds were tiny. Each was just a feathered dot on little legs following behind the mother in a line.

Anise held her breath as they scurried across the way. She didn't want to scare them, and she also didn't want to alert Sebastian and Briac to the bird's presence. She wasn't sure if they would, but she didn't want them thinking of the mother bird as a way to supplement the traveler's diet.

She tried to reach out with her mind and connect with the birds as she had with the chickens at Uncle Sebastian's farm.

She could feel each little spirit and the larger one of the mother bird. Each baby felt like a tiny dot of life, heartbeat, and fear. They were nervous at the open road's exposure, and there was no room for anything else in their tiny minds.

Anise felt a mental 'pop' of disconnection as each little bird scurried into the underbrush on the far side of the road.

"Anise," called Sebastian from down the way. "Don't fall

too far behind."

At each intersection, Sebastian wondered if this would be the point where Briac remembered which way he was heading and left them. He selected the same direction they were going every time by some happenstance.

8

Anise, Briac, and Sebastian were standing on a low hill. Betsy stood a little way behind them. She wasn't as interested in the view as the rest of them. They had left the road and climbed the hill to get oriented, to see exactly where they were.

The view, Betsy's opinion aside, was impressive. There was a busy four-way crossing in the road below them. The road they were following joined the intersection and continued to the gates of a dark high-walled city. Purple flags with a black silhouette of a serpent flew from the battlements. The dark high stone walls curved away to the left of the city gates. To the right, they merged with an imposing rock cliff face. The cliffs towered above the gates and the lower part of the city. They could see that the walls resumed on the top of the cliffs high above them.

Although it was still early afternoon, parts of the lower city were already shaded from the sun by the towering cliffs.

"Grisput," said Briac.

"We're not going in," said Sebastian. "We'll take a route around the city walls."

Briac shivered. "No argument from me."

"But I wanted to see a big city," said Anise.

"Not this big city," said Sebastian firmly.

Approaching the city, the foot and cart traffic on the road increased steadily. As soon as they turned off the main way, it lessened again. The carts with goods, people walking, and troops of guards were more interested in traveling into Grisput than they were in going around it.

The road wound through a wood, drifting further from the city walls as they went. When it began to get dark,

Sebastian suggested that they should find a less well-traveled place to camp. They found a smaller track leading off the main road and followed it for a while.

As they passed some trees on the track, a small village of perhaps fifteen houses came into view. Sebastian heard some sounds and gestured his companions to silence. They crept forward and found a place where they could see what was happening without being seen.

The little town was bristling with armed men wearing tabards with the same purple color and silhouetted serpent that had been on the flags flying over the city walls. Anise started to ask what was happening, but Sebastian held his finger over his lips.

"Grisput guards," whispered Briac.

Sebastian glared at him and repeated his gesture.

The guards were searching the houses. They were everywhere. Sebastian estimated that there were at least two dozen or more. A cart rumbled into the center of the small town. A second one followed it. One of the guards opened the door of the largest building and made a beckoning gesture through the opening.

The guards led a line of manacled people out of the door and toward the cart.

9

The whole population of the town was being loaded into the carts. There were twenty or more people in the chain lines. Anise turned to Sebastian and started to say something. Sebastian repeated his shushing gesture again.

The town looked small and destitute. Sadly, Sebastian thought that there wouldn't be anyone coming to rescue these people. He pulled on the shoulders of his companions, and they backed away from their vantage point.

As soon as they were far enough away that they could talk, Anise said pointedly, "What was going on back there? What were they doing to those people?"

"I don't know, Anise," said Sebastian sadly, "but I can come up with a guess."

Anise waited impatiently for him to continue.

"We avoided going through Grisput because Grisput is one of the few cities in Liamec that supports a system of indentured servitude."

Anise gazed at him blankly. "What's that?"

"It's almost like slavery. If you owe a debt, they make you work to pay it off, and you have to keep working until your debt's paid."

"What debt do those people owe?" Anise asked.

"I don't know," said Sebastian. "Sometimes, they make something up to get free labor."

"That woman on the end of the line, with the red hair, was carrying a baby. How can a baby owe anyone a debt?"

"We don't know the whole story," said Sebastian, "but you're right. Something wasn't right back there."

Briac was watching the exchange. He looked as sad and troubled as Sebastian.

"We have to go back. We have to help those people!"

Anise was almost shouting. Sebastian cast a worried glance back toward the town to be positive they were far enough away that she wouldn't be heard.

"Anise," said Sebastian soothingly, "there were two dozen heavily armed and armored men back there." The calm in his voice just made her angrier. "If we'd approached them to talk, they might well have just added us to the end of the chain. If we attacked them, how long do you think the thistledown in this fine padded jacket you and Isabel made for me would last once they start whacking at me with their swords? I told your aunt and the rest of the town that I would take you safely to the academy. I'm going to do that."

Anise started crying, and Sebastian put his hand on her shoulder.

"Anise," he said gently, "sometimes you have the power to effect change, and sometimes you don't. We're not strong enough to fix this. Life's not fair. The best we can do is use what power we have to make that bit of the world we inhabit a little fairer."

Anise wished she had the power to bring down lightning from the skies. She thought, *One day, I will be strong enough to help people who need it.*

THE CARNIVAL OF WONDERS

1

The light from the fire flickered and reflected off the boulders around their camp. As one traveled around the roads and byways of Liamec, one would often come across circles of boulders with a site for laying a campfire in the middle. It wasn't clear if these had been put together by some age-old traveler's organization or were perhaps magicked into position by wandering mages from the Academy.

Regardless, they were convenient places to camp and often were situated in perfect spots to break one's travel for an evening.

Anise had asked about their progress and how far they still had to go. She'd fallen just a little short of saying, "Are we there yet?" but the meaning had been clear.

They had eaten, and Sebastian was ready to address the question.

He held the map in his hand.

"Well," he began, "we started in Hero. Or, at least some of us did." He nodded to Briac. "We traveled some way due west, leaving the east side of the kingdom and the Blue Mountains behind us."

He looked at the map, met Briac's eyes, and said, "You know, Briac. You're right about this map. It's not very visually pleasing." The spider web of lines representing roads and the dots for towns were helpful for navigation but not very pretty. He pulled a stick from near the fire and sketched in the dirt with it.

He drew a vertical set of inverted v's representing the Blue Mountain range that was the eastern border of Liamec. He followed that with more mountain symbols on two other sides of the map.

"The Etenies mountains border the kingdom to the

south and the west. We've been paralleling the southern arm of the Etenies as we've traveled west."

Sebastian stabbed his stick angrily into the dirt, leaving a divot. "That's Grisput." The divot was northwest of the mark he had made for Hero. "We've been traveling west and north. Ashton and the Academy are here." Sebastian made another mark in the soil. It was near the northernmost end of the mountains in the west.

"Of course," said Sebastian, "the sea is Liamec's northern border." He drew a straight line across the top of his sketch.

Briac leaned over for a closer look at Sebastian's map. "If I was a skilled tracker and saw that set of marks in the earth," he said, with a wink at Anise, "I'd be pretty sure that I'd seen the spot where a pair of rabid badgers made love."

Undeterred, Sebastian continued. "As you can see by the distances on my most excellent map, we're more than halfway. If we skirt around that little pebble, go over or under that twig, we're there!"

Sebastian looked thoughtful. "If we deviate from our path just a bit, about here," he pointed with his stick to a spot near the Western arm of the Etenies, south of the mark that represented Ashton. "We could visit The Serpent's Gorge. It's supposed to be impressive."

"Oh, yes, let's," said Anise.

"I know you're going to Ashton, but are you planning to attend the Academy?" said Briac.

"I think I have to," said Anise.

It wasn't cold, but Briac shivered a bit. "I don't hear good things," he said. "They say people that go to school there come back different."

2

There was a man in the blue tabard of the king's guard coming toward them. Of course, they had encountered the king's guard troops going about their business on the road. They were very distinctive in their chain-mail and tabard. The blue background and the black silhouetted lion's head marked them for all to see and for some to avoid.

Sebastian tried to keep Betsy and his companions on their side of the roadway. They didn't need any trouble with the law.

The man staggered a bit as he walked toward them. Sebastian saw that the guard wasn't much older than him as he got closer. He was also clearly drunk. It was unusual to see a guardsman alone.

As he drew closer to them, he stepped into their path or, more correctly, lurched.

"Are you going to pay the prince regent's toll?" he slurred.

Briac moved forward. "I am Briac, the fabulous," he said. "These are my companions."

The guardsman gave Briac a once-over and said, "Are *you* going to pay the toll?"

Sebastian looked at the man. All musings on being drunk in the middle of the day aside, they didn't want any problems. He sighed and got his coin purse out of Betsy's saddlebag. "I can give you a copper," he said.

The guardsman turned his gaze to Sebastian. "Just throw me the purse."

Sebastian frowned. "No."

The guardsman put his hand on the hilt of his sword. "Throw me the purse," he said. His speech sounded a little clearer with each word.

It occurred to Sebastian that he might have been pretending to be drunk. "No. We need this money for our trip."

The guardsman's sword caught the sunlight as he drew it from his sheath. "Now," he said.

Sebastian drew his own sword and turned his body to angle his right side and his sword arm toward the guardsman. "No."

The guardsman looked shocked at first. He clearly hadn't been expecting resistance. Then, his face broke into a wide smile. The smile made Sebastian feel like he liked the man for a moment. Then, he felt an edge of cruelty underneath it, and whatever illusion of friendliness he thought he had seen vanished.

"We don't have to fight about this," Sebastian said. "Just sheath your sword, and we'll be on our way."

"It's too late for that." The guardsman lunged low and to the right.

Sebastian parried in the seventh position, the years of training with his father serving him in good stead. He hesitated on the riposte, however. He was reluctant to try to injure one of the king's guards.

"Where'd you get such a good sword, boy?" said the man. "That's too good for the likes of you. That looks like a guardsman's sword, or better." He took a mighty swing at Sebastian's head.

Sebastian avoided the blow. It helped, however; it helped in a couple of ways. Despite the guardsman's seeing that Sebastian had a good sword, he hadn't recognized that Sebastian was a worthy opponent. That swing was what you would do if you were fighting someone who had never held a sword before. It also had been powerful enough that it would have taken his head off if Sebastian hadn't avoided it. His opponent was underestimating him and trying to kill him. The underestimating gave Sebastian an edge, and the man's trying to kill him permitted him to fight back.

They met blades a few more times, moving back and

forth on the roadway. Anise and Briac watched anxiously. Briac with his hand on the hilt of his dagger. Sebastian knew he had to act fast. His underestimation advantage wouldn't last if they kept this up for long.

Sebastian didn't hold back on the riposte on the next attack where his opponent over-extended himself. He did, however, try as best he could to hit the man with the sword's side rather than the edge. The flat of his blade smacked into his opponent's head. The guardsman slumped to the ground and lost consciousness.

Sebastian stepped over to the man and checked on him. He hadn't been wholly successful with the flat of the blade. The edge of the sword had given him a cut on his face. It ran from the left side of his cheek, through his lip, and across to below his nose. Sebastian knelt to see if he could stop the bleeding. The cut was probably going to leave a scar.

Sebastian looked around to see if anyone had seen the fight other than Briac or Anise. There was no one on the road except for them. He worried that they would get in trouble with the man's unit. Hopefully, the guardsman wouldn't want his extracurricular thievery to be known. Also, he might not want to admit that a farmer had beaten him.

Sebastian grabbed Betsy's lead and waved Briac and Anise into motion. The best thing they could do was be far gone when the guardsman woke up.

3

A few days later, they reached an intersection where one of the stones had the words 'The Serpent's Gorge' carved into it. The main road led off just a little east of due north. The path marked with 'The Serpent's Gorge' led to the northwest.

That way was more narrow, less traveled, and led up in the direction of the mountains. It looked steeper.

"The Etenies," said Sebastian with some satisfaction. "The snowmelt of the Dragon River comes down from the Etenies mountains, makes its way through the hills, then north, and eventually to the sea. Along the way, as it cuts through the foothills, it carves the gorge. I haven't seen it, but it's supposed to be spectacular. Are we still going that way?"

Anise nodded eagerly. Briac looked stoic. He had told them that he'd already seen the gorge. Sebastian wasn't sure if he believed that. Briac didn't like to admit that he didn't know something or hadn't done something.

They headed off up the trail toward the gorge. Immediately the nature of the trip changed. The major roads in Liamec were well maintained; broad, flat roadways. In some places, preternaturally so. As with the circles of stones that travelers used for campsites, there were rumors that the roads might have been formed or influenced by ancient magics.

The trail they were traveling was more narrow, rougher, and steeper. Betsy was not happy about it. She took to complaining. She didn't voice her annoyance with her mule bray but rather with a constant steady, low grumbling sound. Once Anise knew where it was coming from, it became part of the background noise.

At first, there was no sign of the Dragon River, then there was. The river showed itself and then kept them company for a while. When they first saw it, they took a break for a bite to eat and a wash. The water was cold. Sebastian pointed to the mountains in the distance. "It's snowmelt. That's why it's still so cold even this far from the Etenies."

They filled their water flasks. Betsy took a long welcome drink.

As they continued up the trail, it followed the river at first. Then it took a turn to the left, toward the mountains, away from the roaring waters. They climbed. Betsy's grumbling got louder. The trail switch-backed up a steep slope. As they climbed, Anise caught sight of the river below several times. Each time it seemed more distant.

The trail crested unto a relatively flat plateau. The Etenies towered over the travelers to the west. It felt like the plain extended to the base of the mountain range, but it was a little hard to see through the low windswept trees, rocks, and brush. The pathway turned to the north, crossing part of the plateau.

The travelers walked across the plain. After a while, it started feeling much the same: the same small scrub trees, low bushes, rocks, and dirt. Anise picked a few wild blueberries.

The trail took a slight dip, and their destination came into sight. Anise stopped short. The world dropped away in front of them. At the bottom of the short slope, down into the dip, was the edge of a cliff. Someone had constructed a wooden railing right at the brink. The gorge opened up beyond it.

To Anise, it looked like the other edge was miles away. From where they stood at the top of the rise, the bottom was invisible. The trail they were on led forward toward the railing. Anise thought the path dropped off into the chasm below for a moment. Then she saw a bridge across the gulf, a narrow stone bridge.

The stone bridge must have been formed by magic. It was a single unbroken rock structure. It seemed narrow when they first saw it, but it became clear it was as broad as the roads they'd traveled to get here as they got closer.

There were low barriers on the sides. They were formed of the same stone that made up the rest of the bridge. Anise inched slowly to the corner where the wooden railing on the cliff's edge met the bridge's stone barrier. She didn't think of herself as afraid of heights. Still, this didn't feel like a height; this felt like *the* height.

She peered carefully over the edge. The gorge walls dropped almost straight down. The cliffs were rough brown and gray stone, gradually easing into brown and tan soil and greenery far below. She could barely make out the Dragon River at the bottom. However, It took her a moment to do so because something else distracted her from trying. As she looked below, she tried to understand what she was seeing.

There were spots of brilliant purple of various sizes between her and the greenery around the river far below. Anise blinked, trying to clear her vision. Patches of uniform purple floated between where she was located at the top of the cliff and the bottom. She stared, trying to make sense of it.

Hundreds of feet high, multiple stone columns rose from the gorge's floor. The columns rose to various heights between the river and the canyon's top edge. They were made of a denser stone than the surrounding land. And the purple? The flat tops of the columns had accumulated soil and were supporting fields of flowering purple blossomed thistles.

4

Briac was leading Betsy. She had given Anise a look when Anise handed the lead to him. Skeptical, the expression clearly meant, "He's only been traveling with us for a week. You already trust him with my safety?" When he put a little pressure on the line, she lashed both ears first forward, then back, but she started moving.

Anise walked a little ahead and caught up to Sebastian. She hadn't told Briac about her dreams and why she was going to the Academy. She wanted to share something with her uncle.

"I had a dream last night, Uncle," she said.

"Should I be scared?" said Sebastian.

"It wasn't bad," said Anise thoughtfully.

"So?" said Sebastian.

"I met Helios, the sun god," said Anise. "You told me about him, and I met him in my dream."

"How did you know it was him?"

"In the dreams, you just know," said Anise. "Sometimes. Sometimes you don't. That might be part of what I learn at the Academy."

"So, what was he like? What did you talk about?"

"You were right," she said. "I couldn't look at Helios' face directly. It hurt. I tried at first, but it hurt. Then he took his crown off when he saw me squinting, and it got better."

"So, it was the crown that was bright and not him?" said Sebastian.

"It was both, but the crown was brighter."

Anise paused, then continued, "He was nice but a little strict. He said he might be able to help me later if I needed it."

"That's nice," said Sebastian. He wasn't sure how to take Anise's dreams. They felt like they were something that was beyond him.

"He said his sister said to say, 'Hi,' to you."

"His sister?"

"Selene. The spirit of the moon. We've been calling her Luna."

5

They were passing another circle of boulders when a voice called out. "Ho, the travelers!" A man was leaning against one of the stones. After getting their attention, he sauntered casually over toward them.

He looked young, perhaps between Anise and Briac in age, probably closer to Briac. He was dressed in linen britches and a brown tunic. The thing that struck Anise as he walked over toward them was his hat. The hat was a green felt cap. It had a crimson feather attached to the brim. The red of the feather almost burned in the afternoon sunlight.

"Ya seem a likely group o' travelers," the young man said, smiling. He swept his cap off his head and made a deep bow. "My name is Alan, an' I'm mighty pleased ta meet you." Anise watched, heart in her throat, as the feather in the cap swept within an inch of the dusty road. She didn't want to see that brilliant red color smudged.

Briac bowed back. "Briac, the brilliant. The honor is all ours. These are my traveling companions: Sebastian and Anise." He gestured toward them.

Betsy cut loose with a complaining, "Heee Awwwwwwww!" It was clear to Anise that she was complaining about not being introduced. Briac didn't seem to get the message.

"I'm out here ta greet an' welcome travelers," said Alan. "Welcome ta the Carnival o' Wonders!" He made a flamboyant open-armed gesture of invitation.

Sebastian, Briac, and Anise looked a little confused. There was nothing behind Alan except the circle of boulders. Alan turned and looked. "Sorry," he said. "Let's walk an down the road a bit. I guess I was waiting in the wrong place."

He fell in line with them, and they walked further down

the road in the direction the travelers had been going.

"I'm supposed ta encourage people ta come ta the evening's show," Alan explained. "I'd offer ya discount coupons, except there ain't any. The show's nat very expensive, anyway."

They turned a bend in the road, around the circle of stones. There was a large tent in the process of being set up off the side. People were bustling around driving stakes, pulling on ropes, unrolling canvas sections, and setting up poles. Beyond the workers and the rising tent were rows of wagons: showman's wagons, some of them, and some animal cages.

Alan bowed again and said, "Welcome ta the Carnival o' Wonders!"

6

Alan swept an arm across the air like he was opening a curtain. "The Carnival o' Wonders. Thespians, acrobats, jugglers, dancers, tumblers. We have exotic animals; we have clowns. Our ringmaster is a wordsmith beyond compare. We even have a mime, if ya would believe it, though we keep him hidden inna invisible box between shows."

"Magic?" said Anise, a little breathlessly.

"What's a mime?" said Sebastian.

"And a thespian?" said Briac.

Alan frowned, the lines of the frown momentarily breaking the features of his boyishly handsome face. "Magic! Na magic. Magic is cheating. We use sweat, training, an' talent ta accomplish our magic."

Alan got excited. More so than he already had been. "A thespian is a practitioner o' the dramatic arts. I count myself a member o' this profession." He took another bow: deeper this time.

"We have two wagons in the caravan. We perform a short play during the big show, but we also have a stage set up in front o' our wagons." He gestured over toward the rows of wagons beyond where the tent was being constructed.

Alan shuddered. "A mime is a practitioner of a certain form o' performance called pantomime. He comes from the exotic far-off land o' France. Parlez-vous francais?"

The three just stared at him blankly. Alan shook his head sadly and mumbled quietly, "Liamec. So provincial."

More loudly, he said, "As I said, we mostly keep him in his box."

Alan winked at Anise. "Now, at this point, I'd usually encourage ya an your way and tell ya ta come back later for the show, but ya seem a likely lot. How would ya like the backstage tour?"

7

Alan wanted to show them the animals first. As they walked by the crew setting up the tent, he commented to a man working there, "Good job, Bernhard, but I think ya missed a spot there." He pointed at the spike that the man was pounding into the ground.

If Bernhard wasn't the tallest man Sebastian had ever seen, he was the most muscular. He wasn't wearing a shirt, and the biceps and chest glistening with sweat from the hammer blows were impressive. Bernhard straightened, lifted his massive hammer lightly to his brow, and saluted Alan.

"Bernhard's fresh from Almany," said Alan, "he doesn't speak much English yet. Right now, he's mostly working crew, but he's in training ta be our strong man."

"How'd you get out of working on the tent?" said Sebastian with a smile.

"We need a greeter," said Alan. "Besides, look at me an' look at him."

It was true. While Bernhard was seemingly built of pure muscle, Alan was slight, almost to delicacy. He carried himself well, but it made sense that he might be doing the job he was.

"How old are you, anyway?" said Sebastian.

"Nat that it's any business o' yours," said Alan, a smile undercutting the bite in his words, "but I'm twenty-two." Sebastian was skeptical. Images of kids running away to join the circus occurred to him. He wasn't sure Alan's voice had entirely dropped yet.

They passed the tents and reached the wagons.

"The Menagerie o' Wonders!" called out Alan in a showman's voice.

They were standing in front of two of the wagons in the group. These wagons were divided up into cages with wooden walls separating them. The outer walls were iron bars. Wooden slats could be added over the iron bars for inclement weather.

The nearest cage held a chicken with a hood on its head. There were a couple further on with animals the size of horses. Beyond that, Anise couldn't see what was in the other cages. Alan waved them closer toward the chicken.

"Don't be scared," he said cheerfully. "I'll protect ya."

8

They moved closer to the hooded chicken. An ominous hissing sound was coming from the cage. It sounded to Anise more like a snake than a chicken. "Behold," said Alan, "the mighty Cockatrice!" The chicken turned its head toward the sound of the words.

Anise inspected it more closely. Its belly had scales instead of feathers.

"As ya know, a Cockatrice is born of a serpent hatching a chicken egg. There's supposed ta be death in their gaze." Alan reached between the cage bars and stroked the chicken under its beak. "I call her 'Baby,'" he said. "We think she might be only half Cockatrice. Maybe half Cockatrice an' half chicken? Which would make her three-quarters chicken? Anyway, it's complicated. She doesn't kill ya if she looks at ya; she just gives ya a headache. Rufus is our apprentice in the thespian troupe. He got the job o' Cockatrice victim. Rufus plays dead when she looks at him. He says he wakes up the next day feeling like he's hungover. I told him he's young enough that he shouldn't know what being hungover feels like."

Anise studied the chicken again. Did it have a small leathery-looking tail poking out from under its feathers? She felt grateful for the hood it wore.

The next cage contained a horse. Its backside was turned toward Anise, and it looked to her like an old gray nag. Betsy poked her head over Anise's shoulder to get a closer look.

"Our unicorn, Lucky," said Alan. He came up with a carrot from somewhere and tried to get Lucky to turn around. The wagon stall was just wide enough for Lucky to turn. Eventually, he smelled the carrot and shifted to face them.

Anise was disappointed. Lucky looked just like an old gray mare. The image she had in her head of the spiraling shining unicorn horn from stories was nowhere to be seen. Lucky had a wide squat gray horn on the top of his head. It came to a point and was clearly a horn, but it was nothing like she imagined.

"Lucky's a sweetheart," said Alan. Alan let him crunch on the carrot. Betsy pulled against the lead Anise held, craning her neck to see if Alan had another one.

"We don't think he's a real unicorn," said Alan, "but the horn's real."

The stall next to Lucky's held another animal of about the same size. Anise braced herself for another disappointment.

She was disappointed in her expectation of disappointment. The next stall held an animal, the likes of which she had never seen. It was about the same size as a horse, but black and white stripes covered its body.

"Our hippotigris, Barbara." Alan produced another carrot. Betsy was now clearly expressing her displeasure on her face.

"Barbara is one a' our biggest draws," said Alan. "She comes to us from the far-off land o' Africa."

As they approached the next stall, Anise made eye contact with the creature inside. It was smaller than the horses, about as big as a dog. It was easily the biggest lizard Anise had ever seen. Anise felt intelligence and anger from those eyes that gave her a chill. She thought about reaching out with her mind and trying to touch the creature's presence, but the idea scared her.

"Flambé," said Alan, "our dragon. Keep a little way away from the bars. Sometimes she likes to snap at people."

Like the unicorn, the dragon didn't meet Anise's expectations. She looked like a big lizard, a little potbellied, with short legs and a long thin neck.

"Where are her wings?" asked Anise.

"Maybe she's young. Maybe she's nat really a dragon. Maybe dragons don't fly. I don't know. She's *our* dragon, aren't you, girl?" Alan threw a little piece of meat he got from somewhere through the bars. Flambé's snake-like neck whipped through the air as she gobbled the morsel.

"Besides being an actor," said Alan proudly, "I'm also the carnival's dragon wrangler."

Sebastian had fallen a little behind as he studied the hippotigris. He came up to stand next to Anise and Briac. As he approached the bars, Flambé hissed. The reptile's mouth opened, and along with the sound, which reminded Anise a little of a kettle boiling, a bit of steam came out.

"Huh," said Alan, as he motioned them back from the bars, "she really doesn't like ya." He looked curiously at Sebastian. "I've never seen her react that way ta anyone before."

9

Alan pulled them on past the menagerie to the thespian area. Two carnival wagons were positioned side by side. The front sides of both wagons were pulled down on massive hinges and connected to form the boards. The backstage area of the stage was the interiors of the wagons.

There were people on the stage. They were rehearsing a performance.

"The thespian troupe is the heart an' soul o' our carnival," said Alan with a certain self-satisfaction. He frowned. "Though, I guess some might argue that that back there is the heart." He gestured back toward the people setting up the big tent. "Well," he said philosophically, "at least we have the soul. Tragically, I don't have a part in this part o' the play."

There were rows of chairs already set up in readiness for the evening's performance. They sat to watch.

The scene being played was a duel. It was for the heart of a young maiden. The battle was exciting, though Sebastian couldn't help but notice the difference between the stage fighting and genuine fencing. The goal was often to hit the opponent's sword instead of the opponent.

Anise found her attention drawn to the hero and heroine of the piece.

The heroine was riveted by the duel, unsure if her hero would win or die. She was a picture of innocence; blonde, beautiful, youthful, and petite.

The hero was dueling for his life with his opponent, the villain. He was the most handsome man Anise had ever seen. Tall, with a presence that filled the stage, he had a thin mustache that set off his piercing eyes and noble nose.

Anise found herself as riveted to the performance as the

heroine was to the duel.

Alan leaned over to her and whispered, "He wears lifts."

When the scene ended, the actors left the stage. The petite actress that played the heroine walked down the rows of seats toward them.

"Alan," she called out happily, warmly hugging him.

"Rufus," said Alan with a smile.

"Rufus?" said Anise.

The blonde woman reached up and removed her beautiful curls, revealing a short-cropped head of red hair.

"At your service," said the young man with a bow.

"I think I mentioned Rufus," said Alan. "Our cockatrice victim."

The young man with the short red hair in the stunningly beautiful dress clutched his chest. With a low moan, he fell to the ground and died.

Alan seemed not to notice. "If ya have a moment, we could stop by the pub before I have ta start getting ready for the show tonight," he said.

"Sure," said Rufus from the ground.

10

The pub was another of the wagons. The hinge on the front wall of this wagon was at the top. The wall lifted out to form a roof over the seats and small tables set up in front of the wagon. "Grab a seat," said Alan. He walked over toward a counter.

Anise, Briac, and Rufus settled into chairs around one of the tables. Sebastian found a place to tie up Betsy's lead, where she'd be out of the way, and joined them.

"So, what's special about you lot?" said Rufus.

People were sitting at the other tables. Anise found herself staring. The performers had already started getting ready for the show. They were all manner of people and were dressed in all kinds of outfits. Anise found herself lost in spangles, colors, faces, and figures. Acrobats dressed in skin-tight sequined costumes, clowns, she thought she saw someone who must be the ringmaster, it started to feel like too much, and she looked down at the ground under the table.

"What do you mean?" said Briac.

"Alan's spending a lot of time with you. He must have seen something he liked in you. What was it? I must know." Rufus winked at Briac.

Anise looked up. "Why were all the people in the play, men?"

Rufus frowned. "Some misguided people don't think much of actors or acting, especially when women do it. In England, it's against the law for women to be thespians."

Alan walked back to the table as Rufus spoke. He was carrying a tray loaded down with ale mugs. He set one down in front of each of them.

"I watered yours down a little, young lady," he said to Anise, smiling.

He sat down. "As Rufus said, there are lots o' people who don't think women should be actors."

Alan took a sip of his ale. "If ya all don't mind, I'll just slip into something more comfortable." He reached behind himself, quite agilely, and loosened something in the small of his back, then reached up, pulled off his cap, and shook his head.

Alan's chest seemed to expand, and at the same time, long silky hair cascaded down from under the cap.

Briac found himself staring with fascination at this process. Like a farmer watching the first shoots growing on a newly sown field, the expansion of Alan's chest was, to him, the bursting forth of new life from a formerly barren waste.

And the hair. Briac gazed at it in wonder: Chestnut, caramel, umber, walnut, russet, he couldn't figure out which color it was. It draped over Alan's shoulders like a silken mane.

"Pleased to meet you," said Alan, holding out a hand. "My name's Elaine."

Sebastian took the hand and held it gingerly, with a bemused look.

"I've had to play a man - playing a woman, a couple of times. It gets a little awkward," said Elaine.

"What happened to your accent?" asked Sebastian.

"Alan has an accent. He grew up in the highlands of Errol, in the southwest corner of Liamec. They talk funny over there. I grew up just outside Capitol." Elaine shook her head again, and her hair settled further into place.

Briac tapped Sebastian on the shoulder and whispered, "What color is her hair?"

"Brown," said Sebastian.

11

T he carnival was everything Anise hoped it would be. There was a fair each summer in Hero. At least that's what the mayor called it. People showed off their animals, there was a pie-eating contest and a beauty pageant, but it was nothing like this.

It started with the carnival grounds and the main tent filled with people. Townsfolk from surrounding villages, the people looked familiar to Anise. They were not very different from the neighbors they had in Hero. Elaine explained that, though it seemed to be in the middle of nowhere, the spot where the carnival was set up was carefully chosen. It was halfway between two villages, such that it wasn't a long walk from either.

There were some sideshows. The villagers milled about for a while, looking at the animals, playing games, buying food from booths, and enjoying the sights.

Once they all filed into the main tent, the ringmaster opened the show. Jugglers threw things through the air, and Acrobats walked wires and flew between trapezes. In addition to the exotic animals from the menagerie, there was a horse act and a dog act. When Rufus died at Baby's malevolent glance, Anise cheered. The people sitting near her gave her strange looks.

Anise was unused to being in such a crowded space. She was between Briac and Sebastian, but there were people in front of and behind her. The show was close to sold out. The seats around the ring at the center of the tent were almost all occupied.

The ringmaster *was* the man Anise had seen at the pub. His words filled the tent when he spoke, and there was some kind of magic in them. Anise found herself wanting some of the acts to end so she could hear him introduce the next one.

The thespian troupe came out and performed a short piece about halfway through. Elaine had a female part. She was stunning. Anise observed the beautiful woman and wondered how they hadn't seen Alan for what he was from the beginning.

After the performance, they gathered at the pub again. Happy carnival performers filled the other tables. Rufus was nowhere to be seen, but Elaine got them all ales.

"There's a place for you to sleep," she said. "We've got bunks in our 'guest' wagon. There should be plenty of room."

Sebastian thought about Rufus's question from earlier.

"Thank you so much for your hospitality," he said, "are you sure we can't pay for the tickets for the show, at least?"

Elaine laughed. Briac had his elbow on the table, his chin in his hand, and gazed at her.

"Of course not," she said, "I'm enjoying seeing the carnival again for the first time through your eyes."

The ale kept flowing. Even watered down, it was more than Anise had drunk before. The evening faded into a series of images for her. Was there a time she stood on the strong shoulders of an acrobat, who himself was on top of several others? That image ended in the feeling of falling and strong arms catching her.

Another image was Briac and Elaine laughing at something that Anise didn't think was funny.

She remembered explaining to Betsy that she was very wise not to drink ale, as it made the world spin in an exceedingly awkward way.

One of the last images Anise remembered from that evening was her uncle tucking her into bed in an unfamiliar bunk.

12

When Anise awoke the following morning, she was alone in the 'guest' wagon. She got up and went out to find Sebastian loading Betsy with her saddlebags. He took stock of her, nodded, and asked how she felt.

"Where's Briac?" she asked.

"I don't know," said Sebastian, "I didn't see where he slept last night. I want to get an early start. We can break our fast later."

Briac came out from between two wagons.

"Where've you been?" said Anise, "we need to get going."

Briac shook his head. "I'm not going with you. I played some music for Elaine last night. She said the carnival always needs musicians. She offered me a job."

Anise felt like the ground was dropping out beneath her. She wasn't sure why she cared, but she did.

"Good for you, son," said Sebastian. "Gonna stay with the carnival for a bit, huh?"

"I thought you were traveling with us," said Anise. She tried to sound calm, but she worried she didn't.

"It's an opportunity for me," said Briac. "They have other musicians here, good ones. I'll learn and practice playing with other people." It sounded to Anise like he was rationalizing it to himself.

As they walked out onto the roadway, Briac walked with them for a bit, then stopped, and they paused a little before continuing.

"It's been good traveling with you," Briac said.

Anise felt a teardrop starting to form, so she looked away so he wouldn't see.

Sebastian nodded. They started down the road.

Briac looked sad as well as he watched them go.

Sebastian turned, fished a copper out of his change purse, and flipped it to Briac. "Here you go, son," he said. "For that new lute string."

ASHTON

1

Lakeside, the town on the eastern side of the lake, was a little disappointing. So close to their destination, it seemed an utterly ordinary village, if a little wealthier than Anise was used to. Ashton and the Academy were on the western side. As they left Lakeside, walking along the road that someone from the town had pointed out, Anise was excited for her first glimpse of the lake.

The sun shone through trees onto the road in front of them. The path wound down a forested slope. They had been told there were two ways around the lake. The trail along the north shore was called 'The Wizard's Way' and was less traveled and a little longer than the main track along the southern side of the lake. The southern road was called 'The Peddler's Path.' They had been encouraged to go that way.

The path broke through the tree cover, and the lake was visible to the west. The intersection stood in front of them. It was clear the northern track was less frequently used.

The lake looked clear, cool, and inviting. Betsy immediately started putting pressure on the lead, pulling toward the lakeshore. There was a fourth path from the intersection, a narrow track that led down to the water.

Sebastian didn't see any reason to resist, so they walked down to the lake edge. Anise looked out over the water. The day was bright, the sun shone down, but the middle of the lake was obscured by mist. The other side was shrouded.

Betsy started slurping up the lake water like she had been parched for hours. Anise thought that the sounds that she was making weren't very ladylike.

"Which trail are we going to take, Uncle?" she asked.

"They made it sound like it was obvious that the southern way was for us," said Sebastian with a frown. "It's as if; if you're not a wizard, you're a peddler. But, they did say that it was shorter, so I guess that way makes sense."

As they walked along the Peddler's Path, with the sun gradually lowering in the sky, Anise kept sneaking glances over the lake. The mist in the middle didn't burn off with the warmth.

The day settled, and their way started turning a little north of due west. Anise noticed several threads of thick black smoke rising into the sky. They looked like beacon fires. She pointed them out to Sebastian.

"Ash fires," said Sebastian. "They need ash for the soap. Those fires are probably going a lot."

"Soap?"

"They keep outside of town because of the smell, but Ashton is a major soap production center. Seeing those smoke plumes means we're close."

2

Ashton didn't have a town wall. The road they were on, along the shore, turned away from the lake, and houses and other buildings sprouted alongside it. Without a clear transition, they were in town. Ashton was not a city, but not the smallest town they had traveled through on their way, either. Even in the late afternoon, or perhaps early evening, people, animals, and carts were on the streets.

Anise noticed some individuals among the people making their way through the streets. Not merchants, not regular citizens, they were young and more prosperous than the rest of the populace. She pointed one out to Sebastian.

"A student, most likely," said Sebastian. "They have to have a bit of money, or their parents do, to afford to travel here and attend the Academy. Most of them probably came by coach." Sebastian's tone gave the impression that riding in a coach was an extravagance.

"Rose doesn't have any money," said Anise with concern.

"Lilith made arrangements," said Sebastian reassuringly.

They noticed street signs labeling the street they were walking down, "Main Street." It headed straight toward a hill. The road split into two and curved around the hill's base in both directions. A green, grassy, park-like area was between the street and the hillside. Trails climbed and wound through the park and up the slopes. On the peak of the hill was a crumbling stone tower. The last rays of the setting sun illuminated the stones and made the spire look very appealing.

A watchman carrying a lantern was among the people in the street. Sebastian approached him.

"Excuse me, sir," he said. "Is there an inn nearby?"

"New to town?" said the watchman. He looked Sebastian and Anise up and down. In a not wholly unfriendly tone, he continued, "You're probably looking for something inexpensive."

Sebastian considered taking offense, but instead, he just nodded.

"The Greedy Gull is just down Dead Man's Alley." The watchman pointed. "Don't mind the names; it's probably the best inexpensive inn in town."

"Sir," said Anise quickly, "What's that tower?"

"That's the Dragon Watchtower," the man said. He puffed up his chest to show off his uniform. "I'm part of the Dragon Watch."

The uniform was a leather jerkin and linen britches with a red tabard over the jerkin. In the corner of the front of the tabard, just over the watchman's heart, was a black silhouette of a dragon's head. The watchman was armed with a sword on his belt.

"But the tower's in ruins," said Anise.

"There aren't any dragons anymore," said the man, "if there ever were. Our order's charter specifies that we're supposed to keep a constant watch, but it was a long time ago if we ever did that."

He continued, "Nowadays, climbing that hill is mostly just the first thing that visitors do. There's a nice view of the whole town from up there."

The watchman smiled at them. "Welcome to Ashton," he said.

3

The dining hall of the Greedy Gull was warm and friendly. There was a roaring fire in the fireplace, and the flickering flames cast shadows throughout the room. Sebastian and Anise sat at a table eating stew, which they hadn't had to prepare themselves for the first time in a long time. It was delicious.

"Can we afford this, Uncle?" said Anise.

"Not really," said Sebastian. "Don't worry about it."

The young woman waiting tables in the room came over to them. "Can I get you anything else?" she said. She was just a few years older than Anise. She had tied her blonde hair back in an elaborate set of braids bundled on her head. Sebastian believed that he had figured out that she was the innkeeper's daughter.

Sebastian shook his head.

"Why doesn't Ashton have walls?" asked Anise. "We saw a town that was the same size as this, that had walls, on our way here."

The young woman tilted her head to one side and contemplated Anise. "What good are walls?" she said. "A dragon can just fly right over them."

Sebastian looked at her curiously. "I thought people didn't believe in dragons anymore."

"Well, still," she said.

Anise woke up later that evening. The beds in the inn were surprisingly comfortable. She sat up and looked around the room. There was moonlight shining through the window they had opened to get some air. Her uncle's bed was empty.

She got up, dressed quickly, and crept over to the door. She couldn't think of any good reason why she should keep quiet; it just seemed like the right thing to do.

Still trying to keep quiet, she opened the door and crept down the stairs. The room they had been given was on the second floor up the stairs from the dining hall.

Her uncle was down in the hall, talking to the innkeeper. There were still a few patrons at tables, though it was emptier than when they supped.

Anise crept closer until she found a spot where she could hear what they were saying.

"Is there a weekly rate?" said Sebastian, "I probably need to stay for a week."

"Of course," said the innkeeper.

"You don't, by any chance—" started Sebastian. He paused as if what he was about to say was embarrassing. "Have work available? I'd love to work off the cost of my lodgings."

"Well," the innkeeper started, then he paused also, "our stable boy just quit." His short, well-combed hair was blond, streaked with gray. The similar hair color was part of how Sebastian had recognized him as the waitress's father.

"Yes?" said Sebastian.

"But, you wouldn't want to do his job," said the innkeeper, "it was mostly mucking out the stables."

"I'm a farmer," said Sebastian. "Mucking things out is what I've been doing my whole life."

4

Sebastian and Anise climbed the hill in the park at the center of Ashton. The park's name, The Dragon's Eye, had been on a sign at the gate. The hill was a more strenuous climb than Anise expected. She huffed and puffed a bit. They had been walking every day on their way here, but most of that had been flat. She was glad that Betsy was safe back at the Greedy Gull's stables. They wouldn't have to hear her complain. The morning air felt fresh and clear.

The hillside was forested, and there wasn't a view as they hiked up the gravel pathway. The trees were a mix of pines and birch trees, with a few larches mixed in. To Sebastian, the trees felt different than the ones around Hero. Probably more because of the elevation than being further north. Ashton was in the foothills of the Etenies, and it felt higher and more chilly than Hero.

A few other people were walking in the park, especially closer to the bottom of the hill. Sebastian and Anise just smiled, nodded, and continued on their way.

They reached the top of the hill. There was a clearing around the base of the stone tower. The trees still obscured most of the view, but the trail led right to a dark stone opening that used to hold a wooden door in the tower.

There were ruins of other buildings around the tower's base, overgrown with weeds and vines. The tower still stood, but it had been a long time since it had been occupied or maintained.

Anise ran on ahead, charging into the dark opening. She liked heights, views, old ruins, and exploring, and, though she enjoyed climbing steep hills a little less, this morning's adventure was suiting her fine.

There was a crumbling spiral staircase in the round tower. It wound up the inside of the tower wall. A stone railing was between the edge of the stair and the open central space, but it also was weak in spots and didn't look very stable.

"Careful, Anise," said Sebastian. He had a love-hate relationship with heights. From the bottom, he loved them. From the top, he hated them. Sebastian had inched his way over the bridge at the Serpent's Gorge.

Anise raced up the stairs. The lighting was from narrow arrow slits, and the interior was dark. Sebastian made his way up the tower a bit slower because of the shadows and the crumbling stone.

When he reached the top, Anise was already at the edge taking in the view. There was a broad platform with stone parapets all around. The stonework here was also crumbling, though the town or perhaps the town guard had made some repairs with safety in mind.

"Anise," said Sebastian, "a little further from the edge, if you please."

Sebastian walked over to join her. They were now above the treetops with the tower's height added on, and the view was impressive.

The town of Ashton was spread out below them. Beyond the buildings, the lake was east, and the Etenies mountains, behind Anise and Sebastian, off to the west.

Anise shielded her eyes from the sun with one hand and pointed with the other. "Is that the Academy?" she asked.

A walled-off section with buildings, paths, and green areas was between one part of the town and the lake. The walled-off part and the rest of Ashton had separate waterfronts on the lakeshore.

Streets from town ended at the wall, but Sebastian could see gates.

"I think so," said Sebastian.

Both the town and the Academy felt huge to Anise from here, but she had never seen Hero from above. Perhaps Hero would be even more impressive when seen from a high tower, though she doubted it.

They took in the view for a while, silently. Finally, Anise broke the stillness. "Do we go to the gates of the Academy? What's next?"

"Lilith gave me an address," said Sebastian. "An address and a name—Maeve."

5

After asking around, Sebastian and Anise tracked the address, 13 Leafdrop Lane, to a battered old oak door in an unassuming part of town. The house, one of a row of houses, was painted green.

They would have walked right by if there hadn't been a number on the door. Sebastian hesitated, then knocked firmly. The sun was setting, casting the last rays of its light onto the entryway. Their hike up the hill had taken a little longer than they expected.

The door opened. It took Sebastian a moment to adjust his gaze. The woman opening the door was the most petite person he had ever seen, small in stature but not in presence. Once Sebastian looked in the right direction, he was stunned by bright green eyes and hair so red that it was like a campfire's ruddy glow on a night when someone had pulled the moon out of the sky.

"Can I help you?" she said, looking at Anise, standing a step behind Sebastian. For a second, Sebastian thought that she hadn't seen him because he was too tall.

A sizable open space with brown wooden walls was behind her through the open doorway. The decor and layout of the room reminded Sebastian of a hunting lodge. A few people were in the room, looking with curiosity at the arrivals at the door.

"Um ..." Sebastian started.

"Can I help *you*?" the woman repeated, still looking through Sebastian at Anise. She smiled.

The smile was so warm and open that Anise thought of her mother. The thought made her sad. She squeezed her lips together and made an effort to return to the moment. "I'm supposed to be going to school," she offered.

Sebastian moved out of the way a bit. He felt like his feelings should be hurt, but for some reason, they weren't.

"Of course you are," said the woman. If possible, her smile grew even warmer. She stepped to one side and opened the door wider. "You must be Anise. Come in. I'm Maeve."

THE WAY-HOUSE

1

The room was a common area. There were tables set up for dining on one side next to a kitchen pass-through and an open door frame leading back to the kitchen. The other side of the room had comfortable chairs and benches near a large fireplace.

Two people in the room were watching Anise and Sebastian. One was a man who was probably a bit older than Sebastian, relaxing comfortably by the fireplace. The other was a young woman who ducked down a corridor across from the kitchen, like a startled rabbit, as they entered the room.

The man watched them with open curiosity. He wore a patchwork tunic of linen squares of brilliant colors. He must have had some reason to draw attention to himself, as the tunic did it without difficulty.

"I've been expecting you," said Maeve. "Lilith sent me a letter." She still spoke directly to Anise with a smile on her face. Sebastian wasn't used to feeling invisible.

Two young women came into the room from the hallway on the other side, chattering cheerfully. They were both a little taller than Anise, blonde, and fascinatingly for Anise, identical.

Anise had never seen identical twins before. She'd heard of them, and there were a pair of fraternal twins in Hero, but these two were dressed the same, and Anise was sure she wouldn't be able to tell them apart. They wore blue bodices with light pastel red skirts below. Anise thought they were beautiful.

"Ah, our twins," said Maeve. She raised her voice and called the girls, "Vin, Jord, come over here." She turned to Anise and said quietly, "You might as well start meeting people."

The girls, still chattering happily, started over toward

Maeve.

"They're just starting, like you," whispered Maeve in Anise's ear. "Master Videmon will be ecstatic to have them in his class. He's written papers about his theories about twins."

"Girls," said Maeve, "I'd like you to meet Anise. Anise, this is Vin and Jord." Maeve gestured to one of the girls as she said each name. It seemed that she could tell them apart.

"Anise will be living with us," Maeve said to the twins.

2

The twins appraised Anise. Maeve was waiting for her to say something. Anise turned to Sebastian. "I am?" she said. Sebastian hesitated. He hadn't thought this far ahead. The journey to get them here had filled his attention.

"Of course you are," said Maeve. She pulled Anise to her and tried to envelop her in a hug. It was a little tricky because Anise was taller than she was. "You're part of our family now."

The warmth in Maeve's voice did make Anise feel like part of the family. She didn't even know what the family was, but how Maeve spoke made her feel like she was part of it.

Maeve released Anise and asked, "Didn't Lilith tell you about us?"

Anise shook her head.

Maeve turned to the twins and said, "You'll have to wait a minute for the greetings, girls. We've got some orientation to get through."

For the first time, she acknowledged Sebastian. "What did Lilith tell you?" she asked, looking at him.

"Pretty much just your name and address. And that, we should get in touch with you about getting Anise into the Academy," said Sebastian.

"We'll have to start at the beginning then," said Maeve. She looked disappointed. Sebastian felt like he had let her down personally.

"This," said Maeve, sweeping her arm through the air to cover the room's interior, "is a cunning folk way-house."

Sebastian looked around the room again. The rough wood and simple construction struck him once more. The interior had the feel of a communal living space rather than a private dwelling. The benches, tables, and even the more comfortable chairs near the fireplace look rough and lived-in.

"The cunning folk have a network of way-houses across Liamec. Any cunning folk who need shelter or help can call on a way-house in their time of need."

From the way she was speaking, Sebastian couldn't tell if she included herself as a member of the cunning folk or not.

"Oscar over there—" Maeve gestured toward the man in the colored tunic, still lounging near the fire. "—is staying with us as he passes through."

Oscar gave a wave when Maeve gestured. His clean-shaven intelligent-looking face broke into a welcoming smile.

"This house, though," Maeve continued, "is a little different." She almost lit up as she filled with pride. "We have the additional honor and privilege of passing on students who need that something extra that only the Academy can provide.

"If a cunning person encounters a person with magical potential beyond what they can train, we recommend them to the Academy and, if they need it, house them while they study."

"Recommend?" said Sebastian. A sudden worry filled him.

"We have a relationship with the Academy. The disregard some graduates feel for the cunning folk is not shared by history or all the Academy administration members. In the years this arrangement has been ongoing, neither the Academy nor the cunning folk has had cause to regret it." Sebastian could hear the pride in her voice again as she said this.

3

One of the two blonde girls, impatiently waiting while Maeve spoke, broke in. "I'm Vin. This is Jord. We just got here last week." Maeve looked at her. The expression on her face spoke of patience, but there might have been a whisper of something else underneath.

Anise looked at her as well. Her voice was excited, and her face animated. Anise thought again about whether she could see any difference between the two that she could use to tell them apart. Was there something different in their complexions?

"I'm Anise, and this is my uncle, Sebastian," she said politely.

Maeve broke in. "Vin," she said, "why don't you and Jord show Anise and her uncle what you can do?"

She continued, "As I said, each person that we recommend for the academy has shown signs that they have some unusual degree of talent."

Vin didn't hesitate. She held out one arm and turned her palm upward. A column of flame shot out of her hand and rose toward the ceiling. Anise took a step back in reaction to the sudden heat. She looked with fascination. The flames came out of the air a short distance above Vin's skin. The flickering yellow and orange fire grew from her hand to just a few feet above it.

Lilith had shown Anise some simple elemental magic, but it wasn't Lilith's area of expertise. She was more familiar with alchemy and illusion.

The flames continued to crackle out of Vin's hand. The sound and smell were reminiscent of a campfire.

Maeve turned toward the other girl. "Jord?" she said, a little delicately. Jord stepped forward, more hesitantly than her sister. Anise thought that she might be able to tell them apart by behavior.

Jord lifted her hands and started moving them as if she was forming a sphere. One to the left, a little below, the other above and to the right. Fluid flowed out of her palms. She was cradling a glistening ball of water in her hands in seconds. The campfire smell mixed with another scent that combined salt and a hint of sweat. The skin on Jord's forehead glistened, while Vin's looked dry.

The twins seemed comfortable with this. It was a show they had performed before.

Jord made a throwing motion with her hands, and the ball of fluid flew through the air and crashed into Vin's cylinder of flame. There was a loud sizzling sound, and both the watery sphere and the column of flame vanished, leaving a cloud of steam and a damp, musty smell.

4

Sebastian was still trying to absorb what he had just seen these two young girls do. "Stay here for a moment," Maeve said. "I've got something for you. Let me go get it." She spoke to Anise, "Why don't you girls get to know each other a bit."

"For me?" said Sebastian with surprise.

Maeve crossed the room and disappeared down the corridor across from the kitchen.

Vin turned to Anise and said, "What do you do?"

Anise was confused. "I don't have a job. My aunt's a baker," she started to say.

Vin held up one finger, and a little spurt of flame shot out of it. "No, I mean, what do you *do*!" she repeated.

Jord looked embarrassed.

"Oh," said Anise. She thought for a moment. "Well, I guess I'm a Channeler."

"That's just the one where you dream about things," said Vin. "That's boring."

Jord looked upset. "Vin," she said quietly, "don't be rude." She turned to Anise. "They sent us here when Vin set fire to Mr. Barlow's barn."

Sebastian stepped away from the girls. Perhaps Maeve was correct that they needed to get acquainted. Anise was a little younger than Vin and Jord, but Sebastian was sure she would be able to hold her own. He walked over toward the fireplace and the man Maeve had named Oscar.

"Sebastian," said Sebastian, holding out his right hand toward the man.

Oscar stood from where he had been lounging on one of the benches in front of the unlit fireplace. He held up both empty hands in front of himself. "Oscar," he said with a smile.

"You look a little old to be a student," said Sebastian.

"Well, actually," said Oscar, "the students come in all ages, but I'm not one. Didn't Maeve tell you about this being a cunning folk safe house?"

"Oh. She did. Are you a cunning person?"

"I'm not sure how cunning I am, but I try," said Oscar with another smile. There was a bit of a self-deprecating slant to his smile. One might have called it a wry smile. "Actually, some of the more proper of the cunning folk might call me a hedgewitch, not a cunning person. Don't tell that to Maeve, or she might kick me out." He winked at Sebastian. "You must be new to Ashton."

"We just got in yesterday," said Sebastian. "Traveled all across Liamec. Outlaws, wolves, slavers. It was quite a trip."

"Sounds like it," said Oscar.

Maeve stepped back into the room. She came over to Sebastian and handed him a velum envelope. It had his name on it, and a wax seal sealed it shut.

"That's the seal of one of the masters at the Academy," said Maeve. "Apparently, you have friends in high places."

/

5

A nise took the bottom bunk of a bunk bed in the girls' dorm. Vin and Jord's bunk was on the opposite side of the room. Anise was used to sleeping alone in her room in the bakery back in Hero, and she selected her bed to have a little privacy.

There were ten rough wooden bunk beds in the girls' dorm room. Aside from Vin and Jord, there was only one other occupied bed. Maeve told Anise when she selected her bunk that, the occupancy went up and down. Still, during her time as the way-house manager, the girls' dorm had never been full.

There were several things about the dorms that Anise found noteworthy. There were wooden lockers at both ends of the bed-one for the top occupant and one for the bottom. Maeve explained to Anise that her locker would only open for her. "They're enchanted," she said. "They attune to the person who's sleeping in their bunk."

Earlier, when Maeve had shown her and Sebastian around the way-house, she had waved to the left side of the corridor they were walking down and said, "Boys' dorm room." And then to the right side, "Girls' dorm room."

Anise found herself looking at what seemed like a solid wall on the left-hand side of the corridor, while Sebastian had the same experience on the right. Both of them saw arched open doorways on the opposite side.

"Excuse me," said Sebastian politely. It turned out that Sebastian couldn't even see the girls' dorm room entrance, and Anise couldn't see the boys'.

"It's old magic," clarified Maeve. "This way-house has been here since before my time, and that's longer than you might think." She smiled. She stepped over to what appeared to Anise a blank section of wall and tapped on it. "The boys' dorm," she said. Sebastian was astonished to hear a rapping sound while she knocked on what seemed like an open door frame to him. "And the girls'." She waved toward where Anise saw an open doorway on the other side of the corridor. Sebastian saw a solid wall. "Every so often, we have a student who can enter into both," Maeve concluded.

Later, when Maeve led Anise into the girl's dorm to select her bed, Sebastian watched them walk through what looked to him like a solid wall. He shook his head as he wondered what world he had entered.

The fourth occupant of the girls' dorm was the young woman that Anise and Sebastian had seen briefly when they first arrived. She occupied a top bunk somewhere between Vin and Jord's bunk and Anise's chosen bed. The only way to tell that she had claimed her bed was that her bedding was on it. Anise still hadn't met her officially. She asked Maeve about her.

"Oh, that's my Cian," said Maeve. "She likes to keep to herself." She smiled a little sadly, it seemed to Anise. "You'll meet her when the time is right."

The first night Anise slept in the dorm, she explored the little world that her bunk made between the wood of the upper bed above her, the bed-frames, and the wooden wall of the way-house. The blankets and sheets were warm and soft. The wood of the wall and the bunk was worn down to a shiny polished texture that made it look ancient. There were some carvings and scrapes in the wood. Anise found several names carved into the wall, where she put her pillow. She put her hand on the old worn carved names and felt a connection to the other girls who had long ago slept in this bed.

6

The door was plain and unadorned and not particularly tall. If it hadn't been in the wall that separated Ashton from the Academy, there would have been nothing distinctive about it. Maeve approached it confidently.

"Are you sure this is the right door?" said Anise. She looked up and down the street to see if there was something she was missing. The wall towered overhead, tall and bold. The wall knew where it was and what it was. It was the kind of wall that Anise had been expecting. On the other hand, the door was too quiet and unassuming to be the door that would lead Anise into her new life.

The street also was not what Anise had been expecting. It was almost an alley. The houses on one side and the high wall on the other cut out the sunlight, so it was dark and dingy in the early morning shade. There was no one out this early, and perhaps no one out in this part of town, so it was quiet and empty as well as dim.

Maeve gave Anise a glance. She didn't say anything with her voice, but her eyes, bright green and glowing in the shade like emeralds, spoke to Anise clearly. "If I weren't so polite and nice," those eyes said, "the put down you would be receiving for that lack of faith would make you quake in your little girl boots."

Anise turned her eyes down to her boots. Made by Mr. Fletcher, the cobbler in Hero, they weren't anything to be terribly proud of. They were simple leather boots, worn and dusty from miles of walking. Still, she didn't feel they were anything to be ashamed of either.

Maeve turned her attention back to the door. "There's a whole test thing that the door does on new students," she said. "It checks to see if you're worthy or some such twaddle." She reached out toward the handle. "But, I have to get back in time to shop for the cook for dinner tonight, so we'll just skip that part."

Maeve opened the door, and she and Anise stepped over the threshold and into the Academy.

Anise held her breath. She had the feeling that a new chapter in her life was beginning.

7

Sebastian lifted the shovel load carefully. It was more manageable if you moved the whole load onto the wheelbarrow with one scoop. That way, you didn't have to do a second. The lovely smell of fresh horse manure filled the stall. Sebastian had grown used to the scent over the last few days, though he was more familiar with the perfume of the cow.

As he shoveled, he thought about what had happened since he had left Anise in Maeve's care. Walking away while she stayed behind at the way-house had already been hard. Of course, thought Sebastian, that's the most challenging part of the job for any parent. Sebastian wasn't really Anise's father, but he felt like he was nowadays.

Swen, the innkeeper, was paying Sebastian a bit extra in addition to covering his room and board. He appreciated having Sebastian helping out. His daughter, the waitress in the inn, refused to have anything to do with the stables. Swen had had to do double duty.

Sebastian had had a few interesting conversations with the innkeeper. Swen came from the north and told Sebastian a little about his past.

I wonder how it'll feel when Twilight is old enough to go off on his own, thought Sebastian. He felt a shiver run down his spine. For some reason, the idea gave him a chill.

The letter Sebastian had received was from Lorenzo. He was now a master at the Academy, leading the advanced studies in Channeling. Sebastian had met with him in a pub near the main gate to the Academy the previous evening.

Lorenzo had been pleased to see him. "There you are," he called out. Lorenzo laughed as he shook Sebastian's hand firmly. Sebastian was reminded of the hearty traveling tradesman he had first met on the road years ago.

"Enzo," he said more carefully.

They took a seat at a table in the corner of the dim torch-lit room. Sebastian inspected the man sitting across from him. Lorenzo looked fit. Life at the Academy was suiting him. He looked older than he was in Sebastian's memory. Still, his master's robes from the Academy were elegant and fine and made him seem like a man in charge of his destiny. He still had a broad handlebar mustache, but he had gotten rid of the magical spirals that Sebastian remembered. He was wearing a small jade pendant in the shape of a heart on a leather thong around his neck.

Sebastian had a flash of regret that he hadn't reclaimed that piece of jewelry. It was one of the few things left that had been his mother's. Then he thought about how vital the gem had been to Lorenzo's transformation into the amenable person in front of him.

"How was your journey to the Academy?" said Lorenzo. He had the demeanor of someone getting the pleasantries out of the way before addressing what he really wanted to talk about.

"A bit challenging," said Sebastian. "We barely made it in time for the end of registration."

"That's good. That's good," said Lorenzo distractedly. He leaned forward, looked around at the other tables in the pub without really seeing what he was looking at, and whispered conspiratorially, "I've studied the prophecies again. I think that this is the year. This is the year that the channeler who was predicted to change the world will come to the Academy!"

"That's very exciting," said Sebastian. "I've brought my …" He hesitated before continuing, "… ward, Anise. She's just starting at the Academy, and she hasn't been away from home before."

"Of course. Of course," said Lorenzo. "I'm glad your niece will be joining us." He shook his head as if trying to clear it of other thoughts. He continued, "I've been looking at the incoming students, but it may be hard to identify this channeler. I've also been watching the other realms through my dreams. While I've felt something, it's annoyingly hard to pin down."

"I'm sure you'll figure out who it is eventually," said Sebastian.

8

The room on the other side of the door was huge. As Anise followed Maeve over the threshold into the vast echoing chamber, she felt intimidated. There was a giant face covering the far wall of the room. Otherwise, it was unadorned and unfurnished. Anise first thought the face was a mural.

She thought it was a mural until the eyes turned to look at her, and the giant head leaned forward. The most forceful voice Anise had ever heard boomed, "Who dares enter the presence of the Registrar of the Academy!"

The visage was of a stern, older gray-haired man, and the sound made the air in the chamber vibrate. Anise tried to hide behind Maeve, which was difficult, as she was close to a head taller than the older woman.

Maeve stepped in front of Anise and called out, "Hey, Earl, it's just me, Maeve." She turned toward the face and continued, "You can stop the show."

The giant face vanished. At the base of the far wall was a modest desk with a young man sitting behind it. The desk was littered with an assortment of random papers. Maeve and Anise started across the floor of the large empty chamber toward him.

"What was that?" asked Anise. She tried to sound nonchalant.

"Illusion," said Maeve. "Earl's good at them."

As they approached the desk, Anise dropped into her best impression of a curtsy. She hadn't had to practice curtseys much in the town of Hero, but Isabel had taught her. "Just in case," she had said.

"My Lord Earl," said Anise carefully to the young man sitting behind the desk. He looked young, maybe a year or two older than Anise, and his acne-ridden face froze into an expression of surprise.

Maeve laughed. "Oh, dear," she said, "Earl's not really an Earl. That's just his name."

Anise flushed. Earl's expression of surprise faded, and he looked pleased. "That's never happened before," he said. "I guess, even with the name, I don't look enough like an Earl for anyone to make that mistake." He smiled as he spoke, and the gentle expression warmed his face. Anise didn't quite know where to look. He had a sweet smile, but she didn't want to make him self-conscious about the acne.

"Did you talk to the master healer about that?" Maeve made a gesture toward her face. "As I told you?"

"I tried," said Earl, "but the masters are busy, and I felt there were more important things for the master healer to do."

"Nothing is more important than your health," said Maeve with a concerned frown.

9

Maeve drew Earl's attention to Anise by turning her own gaze at her. "Earl," she said, "This is Anise. She's here to register for the fall semester." Earl stood up from his chair behind the desk. He nodded his head politely to Anise.

"Pleased to meet you," he said. Standing on his feet, he could be seen to be tall, angular, and skinny as a stick. His smile persisted, however, and Anise felt an affinity for him.

"Make it green," she said.

"Huh?" said Earl.

"The face, the head," said Anise, "make it green. It'll scare people more." She met Earl's gaze. "That's what it's for, isn't it?"

"I guess so," said Earl. "Green, Huh? I'll take that under advisement for next year."

"Today's the last day of registration," said Maeve to Anise. She turned to Earl, "Let's get her set up."

"Of course," said Earl. He started digging through the papers that were scattered all over the desk. "She's on my list, right?"

"She should be," said Maeve. "I talked to the masters about her weeks ago."

"Here we go," said Earl as he pulled some papers from under the jumble. "I'm afraid you don't have any choice about your schedule." He looked sympathetically at Anise. "First years don't get much say, anyway, and it's the last day of registration." He handed her a small piece of paper.

Anise looked down at the square of parchment in her hand. Her breath caught in her throat. She nodded. It was just a simple piece of paper with some lines and words on it, but it felt to her like a golden ticket to a new life. She studied it carefully.

She looked up. She felt guilty complaining about something when she should feel nothing but gratitude. Still, the error was so egregious that she had to say something.

"I think that there's a mistake," she said. "Lilith says I need to study channeling, and this has something called clairvoyance on it instead."

Earl shook his head. "That's Master Lorenzo's doing," he said. "It's not a mistake. He's changed some things. Clairvoyance is a new class, and he's changed how you enroll in channeling. You have to find it yourself."

"Find it yourself?" repeated Anise.

"If you can figure out where and when the channeling class meets, you're enrolled," said Earl. "No rules about how except that the other students aren't supposed to tell you."

10

Anise was saying goodbye to Sebastian. It felt like she was dying. With tears streaming down her face, she said, "What if the Watcher finds me. What will I do without you?" She felt guilty about crying, but she couldn't make herself stop.

"The Watcher?" said Sebastian.

Anise sniffed. "Yes, the Watcher. I told you about him."

"Anise," said Sebastian, "you didn't. Someone is watching you?"

"In my dreams," said Anise. "For a while now. He's looking for me more than he's watching me, I guess." She frowned. "I thought I told you."

"In your dreams," said Sebastian. He felt relieved, though he tried not to show it to Anise. "Sometimes bad dreams are just bad dreams, Anise."

"Helios said he'd hide me from the Watcher." Anise smiled through her tears. "I think he likes me."

Sebastian reached out and pulled Anise to him in a tight hug. "Don't cry, Anise," he said. "You'll be fine here. I've asked Maeve to take care of you, and you're excited to start classes, aren't you?"

Anise sniffed again. "Yes," she said.

"You should feel sorry for me," said Sebastian. "I'm the one who has it hard." He looked thoughtful. "Well, Betsy and I. We're the ones who have to walk home."

11

Anise was lying in her bed. The wood of the top bunk was like an additional cover over her. The confinement gave her the sensation of being in a cocoon. Her blankets were warm enough, but she worried about her toes. She lifted her legs, reached down, and folded the bottom edge of the blanket under her feet to create a pouch or pocket for warmth.

She felt she should still be crying and wanted to, a little, but her eyes were all cried out.

It was dark in the dorm. Maeve had called for everyone to put their candles out when the curfew bell rang. There was a church not too far from the way-house, so they felt each peal of the hourly bells.

There was a noise by the door of the room. It was Maeve. Anise saw the candlelight come closer as Maeve walked between the bunks. She pulled her blankets up to her face and watched the glow approach her over the top edge.

Maeve sat down on the side of Anise's bed and put the candle down on the wooden locker at the head. There wasn't much in that locker. Just the clothes Rose had stuffed into one of Betsy's saddlebags as they left Hero, the little pouch of coins that Sebastian had given her, and the little wooden caged bird puzzle Isabel's mother had made.

Maeve reached out one hand and stroked Anise's hair out of her eyes. There was a dried salty tear streak on her face.

"Anise," said Maeve. She assessed Anise's face, licked her thumb, and wiped away a little of the salt with it.

Maeve was holding something tucked under her arm. Anise saw some small portraits or pictures on a folded bundle of fabric in the flickering light of the candle flame.

"I brought you this," said Maeve. She unfolded the piece

of fabric and spread it out over Anise and the bunk bed. It was a quilt. As it settled over her blankets and especially over her feet, Anise felt her worries about her toes fading.

"Thank you, Maeve," Anise said. She looked more carefully at the quilt. It was beige. Each fabric square held embroidered images of dragons in different poses and colors. Anise reached out and felt it. It was soft and felt thick and comfy.

"It's beautiful," Anise said. "And so warm." She wiggled her toes. "What's it made of?"

Maeve looked thoughtful, like that wasn't the question she was expecting. "It's stuffed with thistledown," she said. "I make them for the first years." She frowned a little as she said, "For some reason, I picked this one out for you. Something to do with the pictures."

"Thistledown?" said Anise. "But it's so soft."

"My people have been using thistledown for a long time," Maeve said. "I mean, my family. We have a technique for softening it. It's good against dragons."

Maeve leaned over and kissed Anise on the forehead. She got to her feet and turned to go. "Sleep well, dear," she said.

Anise wiggled her feet again. Her toes were beginning to appreciate her pocket of warmth.

THE ACADEMY

1

Anise, Vin, and Jord approached one of the main gates between the town and the Academy. Unlike the little door that led into the registrar's office, this double-doored gate was wide enough to admit two carts side by side when fully open. It wasn't fully open now. A smaller person-sized door was set into one of the gate doors.

A couple of guards were sitting on chairs on both sides of the open person-sized entry. One of them was leaning his chair back against the gate behind him. The other was staring idly at passersby on the street. The guards looked bored. This street was busier than the little alley outside the registrar's office; people passed the gate to the left and right. However, not many were going through the door between the two guards.

Like the watchmen in Ashton, the guards were dressed in leather jerkins and linen britches. The tabard that they wore over the leather was black. Also, like the watchmen, they had a silhouette stitched into the fabric just over their hearts. The symbol, shown in white to be visible on the black of the tabard, was an owl's head.

Vin, as she had all morning, took the lead. She strode decisively over toward the guards. Anise and Jord followed.

The guard who had been people-watching looked up at Vin, "Can we help you, ladies?" he said. The other guard leaned forward on his off-center chair. The back moved away from the gate wall, and he balanced on two chair legs for a moment before the front legs dropped to the ground with a thud.

Maeve had been the one who had suggested that Vin and Jord take Anise along with them into the Academy. It would be their second expedition. They had already toured the campus once, learning where their classrooms were and how to get around. Vin had not looked too happy at the suggestion.

"You're all first years," Maeve had said. "You're probably in most of the same classes, anyway."

The late morning sun shone down on Anise's back as she watched Vin talking to the guard. She felt like Helios had his arm around her shoulders.

The guards didn't seem surprised to see them. It was the last sun's day before classes started, and there had been lots of students going back and forth. The guards took a quick look at their schedule cards and waved them on.

As they stepped through the doorway onto the Academy grounds, Anise held her breath. She hadn't thought about this place much while growing up, but she'd certainly been thinking about it for most of the trip with her uncle to get here.

Her first impression didn't disappoint. The sun was shining down on an immaculate green crisscrossed with gravel walkways that cut across it at every conceivable angle. There were stone buildings on both sides of the broad green and another tall one at the far end. It had a tower that sported a clock and a belfry.

People walked on the paths across the green. Some were in groups, walking together, and some individuals were walking alone. Anise watched one man in a black robe, which she took to be master's garb, walking hurriedly across the green on one of the gravel paths. He was looking at the ground in front of himself, muttering distractedly. He hardly noticed others that crossed his path.

The bell in the tower rang right as they stepped off the cobbled road that ran between the wall and the green and walked onto one of the gravel trails.

"Sext," said Vin with satisfaction. "That gives us some time." She dismissed Jord and Anise with a glance. "You two try to find your classrooms." A slight smile crossed her lips. "I'm going to see if I can find someone interesting to talk to." She took off down one of the gravel ways, leaving Anise and Jord looking at each other.

Vin and Jord had dressed similarly again today, though Anise was starting to feel that telling them apart wouldn't be so hard after all. They wore blue linen smocks, but Vin had hers tightly belted at the waist, while Jord wasn't wearing a belt.

The main reason, though, that Anise thought she would be able to tell them apart was by their behavior. Vin radiated an intimidating, fiery self-confidence. Jord was more easygoing.

Jord sighed and looked down at her schedule, which she still held.

"Is your first class on Moon's day morning: alchemy?"

2

Anise awoke in her bed. She considered the wood of the top bunk above her and wondered what time it was. The dorm room had windows on the wall opposite the doorway into the hall, but they were north-facing, so they never got direct sunlight.

The lighting felt strange. Anise sat up and looked around. The room was dark, except for a slight warm glow that reminded her of late afternoon sunlight on a sleepy autumn day. Except for hers, the room was empty of bunk beds. The open space made her realize how large the dorm was.

A man stood a few paces away from her. He was the source of the gentle glow of sunlight. The light was coming from his body, clothes, and hands, but the brightest rays came from his face and the golden crown atop his curly blond locks. He wore a purple mantle draped over one shoulder and across his chest. It was belted at the waist by a broad silver band with glowing images depicting the zodiac signs.

"My lord Helios," said Anise. She knew enough to be respectful to certain people in her dreams. She could issue orders to some of them; for others, she felt the need to listen when they spoke. Helios was in his own class. Anise was careful to afford him every courtesy she knew.

"Anise," he said. "I've been keeping an eye on you."

"Don't you watch us all," said Anise, "from your place on high?"

The golden-haired god laughed. It made him look even younger than he had at first. The sound of his laugh was a merry ringing noise. The rays of light in the room shook and trembled with his glee.

"I suppose so," he said. "But," and here, a sober look shadowed his proud face, "I'm not the only one."

"I know," said Anise. She shivered a little. "The Watcher."

"I can keep his gaze from you a bit," said the god. "I can distract him with other things to see. But, it would be better to avoid the places where he is focusing his attention."

Anise waited patiently. It was clear that Helios wasn't done, and with him, she had determined that it made him happy to know that he was being listened to and respected.

"He's watching the students at the Academy," continued Helios. "Especially in channeling classes." He looked thoughtful, in as much as his shining face was capable of looking thoughtful. "I was going to tell you where and when the first channeling class will be held, but I think I'll tell you about the second class instead. It'll help keep his gaze off of you."

"Thank you, My Lord," said Anise. "I appreciate the help. But, I wonder, why me? I didn't even try to dream of you tonight." Anise frowned. *I didn't try*, she thought, *but perhaps I did it by accident. Maybe I do need control.*

The god laughed again. The sound of his laughter made Anise feel like her ears were warm, as the rays of light emanating from him made her body warm. He turned his gaze fully upon her. Her forehead and cheeks felt flushed. His eyes weren't any color; they were just the warmth and fire of light.

"Anise," he said. "I know you can't see it yourself, but here in the dreaming realm, you glow and shine as I do. You remind me of myself."

3

The skin on Anise's forehead felt tight. It itched and burned a little. Maeve had spread a little honey over Anise's brow and cheeks when she noticed the reddening in the morning. "How did you manage to get a sunburn since yesterday?" Maeve asked. She didn't wait for an answer. Anise's face still felt sticky.

She and Jord were sitting in chairs at the back of a classroom. Vin had strode in confidently and immediately found a seat toward the front next to a girl dressed elegantly in purple. They struck up a loud conversation. Anise and Jord drifted quietly toward the back row.

"I'm not sure how she does it," Jord whispered to Anise. "She just seems to know what to say and when to say it."

Anise nodded and pointed toward a door on one side of the front of the classroom. The master was arriving.

The classroom wasn't huge. There were rows of seats with desks for the students and a podium at the front for the master. The walls were lined with cabinets and bookshelves. Jars of interesting-looking and sometimes creepy things sat on the shelves. Herbs and spices hung on hooks from the ceiling. Anise wished she had more time to look around the room. Perhaps she would have some time after class.

The master stepped through the door. He was the oldest man Anise had ever seen. She got the sense that his body was skeletal under his black master's robes. Wisps of white hair stuck out from both sides of his head. He leaned against the door as he closed it, then shuffled slowly over to the podium.

"Greetings, class," he said from behind the podium. His voice seemed as old as the rest of him. High and reedy, it felt like it might blow away in the wind if a window were left open. There was a large slate fastened to the wall behind the podium.

Anise had never seen such a thing before. Written in white on one side of the black surface of the slate was the name Master Ernst.

Jord leaned over to Anise. "You know what Vin heard?" she whispered conspiratorially, "She heard that he's older than the Academy. When they came here to break ground to start to build, he was waiting for them."

Master Ernst began, "Alchemy is sometimes dismissed. Not as flashy as elemental magic or illusion. No bolts of fire shooting from your fingertips. No images of dragons flying through the sky." His voice was reedy, but it fought a path through the room to the furthest chair.

"Look at me," said the old man. Delicate though it was, Anise felt his voice conveyed information that she wanted to hear. "How old do you think I am?"

Several hands in the class went up.

"That was a rhetorical question," said the master. "I don't care what you think. I'm three hundred and seven years old." There were gasps from some of the students.

Jord leaned over to Anise again. Anise struggled with her attention, as she was interested in what Master Ernst was saying, but she didn't want to be rude to Jord.

"Vin heard," Jord whispered, "that he's been asking the same question in each introductory class for twenty years, and he's said three hundred and seven each time."

4

The master continued, "Potions. They can have lasting permanent effects on the world. A bolt of fire or shifting of the earth can impact things. Channeling can erratically cause events. But, if you want a consistent, reliable way to make changes, particularly changes to people, give me alchemy every day. Don't even get me started on illusion; the definition of impermanence.

"I can brew an elixir that will cause you to grow a tail. I can concoct a draught that can make you fall in love. I can prepare a mixture that melts iron. Nothing in any other discipline you will study here at the Academy will be as permanent and lasting as what you learn in this class.

"Alchemy is disrespected in some ways, but it is respected in others. My potion of health, which has allowed me to live to my hale old age, is favored by the Kings of Liamec. Have none of you ever wondered how the reign of King Liam II could have lasted a hundred years?

"If you grasp what I teach and do well, you too will be able to change the world with your powerful brews and concoctions."

The Alchemy master removed a small vial from a pocket in his black master's robes. He held it up in the air. The glass of the vial, or perhaps the fluid inside it, was colored pink. The facets in the small bottle caught the morning sunlight and glittered prettily.

"You'll hear a lot about Keys here at the Academy if you haven't already," the aged master said. "A Key, as we use the word here, is a thing, a place, and an idea simultaneously." He made a small gesture with the vial to draw the student's eyes to it again. "This, the fluid in this vial, is the Key to Alchemy."

The master put the vial back in his pocket. "The Key to

Alchemy is also, at the same time, a place and an idea, but we will cover those aspects of it another time."

Jord searched Anise's eyes. "Vin heard about the Key to Alchemy," she whispered. Anise looked at her and lifted her eyebrows. "No," Jord shook her head. "I'm not going to tell you; it's too gross."

"You'll all be getting vials like the one I just showed you," said Master Ernst, "next time." He shook his head as if the thought of the students all getting those vials was too much. "Be very careful with them. One drop is all you need for each potion."

"I suppose you're wondering why we have class so early in the morning," the master continued. "Alchemy is best and usually practiced during the daylight hours." The master looked thoughtful. "There are some exceptions. Some potions require moonlight, and some need an absence of light. Still, for the most part, sunlight is a cleansing agent, and the freshness of a morning yields an unsullied liquid and an alert alchemist."

5

The residents of the way-house ate dinner together. Not always, and not everyone sat at the table every time. Still, as a rule, when the town bells rang Vespers, there was food available, and Maeve's charges would be there to partake.

Since Sebastian had left on his return journey to Hero, Anise had met the other residents of the way-house. In addition to Vin, Jord, and Maeve herself, four other people lived there.

Anise, who was used to eating at the bakery with just Rose for company or eating with Aunt Isabel and Uncle Sebastian, found the crowded evening meals fascinating.

Oscar, of course, who Anise had been introduced to when she arrived, was one of the four. Cian, who Maeve had referred to as "her" Cian, was quiet and kept to herself, though she ate with gusto and relished her meals.

The cook, who they all called Cookie, didn't live in the way-house. He was a burly man with a large brown mustache that turned down at the corners. It looked a little sad to Anise. Not that it was a poorly maintained mustache. It was well-groomed and must be Cookie's pride. No, it was just that the downward turning corners made her think of a frown and reminded her of grief.

The cook's boy, who helped in the kitchen, lived in the way-house. Apparently, he had no other place to live. Maeve told Anise that Cookie had rescued him off the streets. Anise tried to find out his name, but no one knew it. "He's just the cook's boy," Maeve said. He seemed like he might be a few years younger than Anise. He was skittish and jumped when anyone moved too near him.

Both Cookie and the cook's boy would sit with them and

eat after serving. There were two large wooden tables in the dining area of the common room. There was enough room at either of the tables for the whole group to sit at the same one. They spent some dinners that way, but sometimes, one diner would choose to sit alone at the other table. This was usually Cian, or Niall, the final resident of the boys' dorm.

Niall, like Cian, liked to keep to himself. The first time Anise saw him sitting at the dining table, she had difficulty breathing for a moment. He was tall, dressed simply in a green tunic, and strikingly handsome. He was an upperclassman. He was at least a few years older than Anise. He hardly said a word that first mealtime, but she covertly snuck glances at him several times.

6

Anise had found herself sitting next to Oscar during her first meal at the way-house. His patchwork tunic of brightly colored linen squares struck her again. The colors flickered and flamed in the setting sun's light pouring in through the windows.

"Anise, right?" he asked.

Anise nodded.

"Oscar," said Oscar. He held his right hand out briefly, palm outward, fingers pointed toward the ceiling.

"I know," said Anise, "Maeve told me." The house matron watched the conversation from the other side of the table.

"How're you settling in?" asked Oscar.

"I guess I'm a little homesick," said Anise. She considered Oscar and returned the question. "Are you a student? You look old."

Oscar laughed. "I wouldn't have them, and they wouldn't have me," he said. "I'm just passing through. Didn't Maeve tell you about the cunning folk safe-houses?"

"I guess she did," said Anise.

"Your uncle told me about your trip to Ashton," said Oscar. "It sounds like it was quite an adventure. He said something about wolves and outlaws."

"Oh, the wolves weren't anything," said Anise, "That was just a bad dream I had. The outlaws were a little scary. They shot arrows at us."

"They didn't try to hurt you, though, did they? Probably just looking for money."

"They said they weren't allowed," said Anise. "They said they were only allowed to take money from the Young Lion's tax collectors and rich people."

"Well," said Oscar with another smile, "Imagine that, outlaws, with a conscience."

7

Vin and Jord weren't in Anise's illusion class. Cian was, however. When Anise saw her seated in the classroom, she thought briefly about sitting next to her. But, she was almost sure that Cian had seen her walking across the green, and had avoided eye contact, so Anise wasn't sure she would be welcome.

Vin and Jord weren't in the illusion class because they were taking a required course on literacy. The town of Hero had a surprisingly advanced education system for Liamec. The most progressive part of the system was that it existed. The incoming class of students at the Academy were more educated than the vast majority of citizens, but only about half could read. Anise hadn't taken a test, so she wasn't sure how the registrar had known that she could.

The classroom was similar to her alchemy classroom. There was a podium in front, a desk beside it, and a black slate on the wall behind.

She found a seat in a back row, not next to anyone, and waited for the master to arrive. A person stepped up to the podium at the front. The name Master Devona was written on the black slate behind her. At first, Anise was a little confused as to what was happening. Was one of the students playing a prank before the master arrived? The person behind the podium looked more like a girl than a woman. Certainly, not like a master. She hardly looked older than Anise herself.

Anise studied her. She stood on a box, or perhaps two, raising herself to the level of the top of the podium. She was probably no taller than Cian, if not a little shorter. She had curly blond hair that fell in ringlets to her shoulders and a face that was as bright, sunny, and pretty as a porcelain doll.

The girl cleared her throat. The eyes of the students in

the room turned to her, and some of the chattering stilled.

"Hello, class," she said, "I am Master Devona. Welcome to the world of illusion!" Her voice reminded Anise of a warm spring day and happy times from her childhood.

The master scanned a piece of paper on the podium. "Anise," she called out loudly, then looked up expectantly.

Anise's heart started beating strongly enough that she felt it would bounce out of her chest. *Could she have already done something wrong to be called out in front of the class in the first session?* The master was scanning the room as if looking for her.

Anise slunk down in her chair, trying to appear invisible while at the same time raising her hand. The master spotted Anise's hand and marked her parchment with a quill pen. She called out, equally loudly, "Cian?" and looked up again.

Anise's heart started beating again. She had missed the moment when it went from beating like a drum to stopping, but it started back to normal now. The master was taking attendance.

A young man sitting in the second row spoke up. Anise disliked him on sight. He slouched on his seat and had his legs draped over the chair in front of him. "My parents aren't paying good money to have little girls teach me," he said.

Almost nonchalantly, the master waved her hand in his direction. She hardly looked at him. Anise gasped, as did most of the people in the room. A lion appeared in front of the first row of chairs, charged forward, put its paws up on the desk the young man's legs were on, opened its jaws, and roared, shaking the room.

The young man fell off his chair and tried to hide under the desk. Anise looked again at the lion, who had started sniffing around the seat. It looked a little transparent at second glance, though it didn't look like the young man thought so.

Master Devona waved her hand again, and the lion disappeared. Anise thought she caught a whiff of its scent as it vanished.

"What I've just demonstrated," said Master Devona calmly, unfazed by the interruption, "is a targeted illusion. There's an aspect of illusion that allows a connection with the subject's mind."

The master finally met the eyes of the young man, and Anise thought she caught a hint of a smile. The young man climbed out from under his seat and sat back down. He was breathing as if he had just run a marathon.

"When a skillful illusionist targets an illusion," said Master Devona, "an image will be selected that comes from the target's fears and anxieties. The illusionist may not even know what image is being created."

The young man lifted his hand timidly. "Master Devona," he said, "Might I be permitted to visit the restroom?"

8

Anise was finding the solid wooden boards a little uncomfortable. She sat, cross-legged, on the polished oak common room floor. Around her were the other residents of the way-house. Many were fidgeting like Anise, trying to get comfortable.

They were seated in a circle, all on the floor, facing each other. At the head of the group was Maeve, practically glowing in anticipation. The afternoon sunlight was shining in through the windows. Bands of light dappled the oak floor.

The door to the outside opened, and someone started to walk in.

"Oscar," called out Maeve cheerfully, "Come and join us."

The door stopped, then moved back and forth as if whoever was on the other side was unsure which way to go. Finally, it opened further, and Oscar stepped into the room.

"It's Woden's day, isn't it," he said sadly.

"It is," said Maeve happily. Her smile widened.

Oscar resignedly came over to join the circle. Cian and Jord moved aside a little to give him room to settle on the floor between them.

"Now," said Maeve. "For the benefit of those new to the house," She eyed Anise as she spoke, "I'll explain what we are doing sitting here on the floor."

Anise looked around at the circle of faces. Looks varied, but they mostly seemed resigned. Vin and Jord were sitting next to each other. By now, Anise could tell them apart without difficulty when she saw them together.

Cian, Niall, and Oscar all shared the same expression. They were the prisoners who had accepted that there was no way to avoid their fate and went to the gallows, determined not to show weakness.

The cook's boy was sitting between Anise and Maeve. He looked like Anise felt: worried and unsure. If Anise had known him better, she would have put her arm around his shoulders.

"On Woden's day," said Maeve, "we enjoy a moment of peace and companionship, where we share our feelings and talk about our lives. A little thing that I call the time of the circle."

Maeve grinned like a cat that just caught a bird. "Oscar," she said, "Seeing as you were so enthusiastic about joining us, maybe you can get us started." She turned to Anise and continued, "During the time of the circle, we take turns talking about things that we are grateful for."

"Well," began Oscar. The patches on his shirt caught the light streaming in through the windows. The bright colors of the linen squares glowed in the warm afternoon sun. Anise wondered if he had multiple shirts with the same design or always wore the same one.

"I'm beholden to Maeve for maintaining this wonderful house and giving me a place to stay," said Oscar. Maeve was shaking her head and frowning. "And, I know that's the same thing I said last week," he continued. He looked thoughtful.

"I'm grateful that the world affords a wandering man so many interesting possibilities. I'll be leaving you all soon to try to find my next adventure." Oscar smiled. "Maybe something political this time."

There were murmurs of regret at Oscar's announcement, but it didn't come as much of a surprise to the long-term residents. Oscar had been at the way-house for several weeks, but he had always said he was passing through.

Maeve pointed to each resident in turn after Oscar. Most shared some form of the same gratitude about the existence of the way-house. With the warm sunlight flooding the oak floorboards and warming her back, and with the presence of the circle of people around her, Anise started to feel closer to her fellow residents.

When it was her turn to speak, she overcame her nerves and talked a little about how excited she was to be at the Academy. About how much she was looking forward to learning. And, finally, about how welcome she felt at the way-house.

It turned out that the cook's boy was named Raphael. When he spoke, he quietly shared how grateful he was to have a place to sleep and enough to eat. He was thankful to Cookie for offering him employment and Maeve for the roof over his head.

THE HALL OF ELEMENTS

1

Jord and Anise walked together to Elements class. Vin had started keeping company with some girls she had met, and neither Jord nor Anise felt welcome to join them. As they approached the stone-walled building that their class was in, Anise took a moment to look at it.

The building was huge; it towered over the adjacent structures. It was also broad as well as tall. Anise had seen it before when walking to her classes. It was impossible not to see it. The building occupied more than its fair share of the Academy grounds. She had had to trek around it several times over the last week.

"The Hall of Elements," said Jord quietly. She gazed at the stone wall looming above them with admiration and apprehension.

Anise had a flashback to climbing the tower in the Dragon's Eye park with her uncle. She remembered seeing a huge building in the center of the place they had identified as the Academy. Even though it seemed vast from the tower top, it looked even larger standing below it.

"This should be the classroom," said Jord, pointing to a door. The door was dwarfed by the height of the stone wall above it.

As they opened the door and stepped into the room, it struck Anise as different from her previous classes' rooms. There was still a Master's podium at one end of the room, with a slate board behind it. There were still rows of desks for the students. But, the room was narrow and long, with one side having windows opening out onto the green walkway outside the building and the other side a windowless inner wall. There was only one doorway other than the one that they were entering. It was as if the room was an afterthought in a building that was thinking about something else. Like the building's wall had been made a little wider here, and the classroom stuffed into it. The one other exit was a narrow door on the windowless inner wall. Made of solid metal, the door shone as if polished. There was a massive lock just below the door handle.

Anise glanced around the room. Though narrower than the other classrooms, the walls on both sides were still lined with bookshelves and cabinets. On one shelf, she saw a glass jar that contained a whirlwind. Small feathers were spinning around in the sealed jar, swirling continuously in a spiral.

Anise didn't have much time to think about it as the master of the class was leaning on his podium, intently watching the two of them walk through the door into the classroom.

"Vin and Jord?" he said.

2

Jord looked up, raised her hand, and walked carefully toward the master. Anise followed. Not in response to what he had said, but because she planned to sit beside Jord in the classroom. The master studied them as they walked toward him. The expression on his face changed from attentiveness and interest to disappointment as Jord, with Anise following, advanced down the central aisle between the rows of desks.

Anise looked back at him. With an effort, she kept her mouth from opening in shock. The master's skin was dark. Darker than anyone she had ever met before. She hadn't known that anyone's skin could be that dark.

"You were supposed to be identical twins," said the master sadly. He was about average height. His tightly curled dark hair peeked out from under the black master's cap he wore, matching his robes. "You don't even look alike." He spoke with a trace of an accent that Anise couldn't place. Though if the truth is told, she hadn't heard many accents until visiting the Carnival of Wonders.

"Oh," said Anise. "I'm not Vin." She looked around. "I guess she's not here yet."

The master looked relieved. "That's good then," he said. "Grab a seat, and we'll get started." He looked up and scanned the class. "Welcome to Elementary Elements," he said.

The door opened, and Vin entered the room. She was in the company of the girl wearing purple who she had met in alchemy class. The master glanced at them, paused while they found seats, and continued. "Some words of introduction are in order. I am Master Videmon," he gestured to his name on the slate.

"I hail originally from the empire of Mali in the African continent," the master went on. There was a bit of a murmur in the class at this. "I learned my knowledge of the elements in the libraries of Timbuktu."

One of the young men sitting toward the front of the class raised his hand. The master nodded at him in acknowledgment.

"Master," said the young man, "Did you ever meet Prester John?"

Master Videmon laughed. "Prester John?" he said with a smile. "Africa is big."

He continued, "And, after all, I'm not sure Prester John would want to meet someone whose only minor skill is being able to do things like this:"

The master lifted his hand in a gesture eerily similar to what Anise had seen Vin do what felt like a lifetime ago. A column of flame shot up out of his hand. He then moved his other hand in a spiraling motion around the column. A water trail formed a glistening spiral around the flame, flowing as if streaming through the air. All the air in the room was being sucked toward the fire and the water. Anise felt a wind flowing past her face.

Master Videmon snapped his fingers on his left hand. Several steel spheres, lying on his desk, leapt into the air and started circling the flame and water construction.

The master stared fiercely at his creation. In addition to the wind, Anise felt all the moisture being sucked out of the air.

Master Videmon relaxed, smiled at the class, and waved his hand. The structure vanished with a hissing sound, and the steel balls clattered to the floor.

3

Maeve was leading an expedition. Jord, Cian, and Anise followed her like ducklings following a mother duck. They walked down Leafdrop Lane away from the oak door of the way-house. The sun's light showed signs of starting to withdraw to the west.

Jord and Anise walked side by side, just a step behind Maeve. Cian was bringing up the rear. Vin had asked to be excused; she had a rendezvous scheduled with a friend.

Anise was excited. She hadn't been to the bathhouse yet. They each carried a linen towel and a canvas bag to keep their belongings in while they bathed. Maeve had a lantern to light for the walk home.

"Is it just people from the Academy who are allowed to use the bathhouse, or can people from town use it also?" she asked.

"Just the Academy," said Maeve casually.

Anise wondered again exactly what Maeve's relationship with the Academy was. She was afraid to ask.

As they approached the Academy gate, the two guards on duty stood up from their chairs beside the door. "Maeve," said one with a nod. The other opened and held the door for them. Though they had been relaxed in their chairs, their black tabards were clean and neat, and they seemed alert.

The bathhouse was down nearer to the lakeshore than Anise's classrooms. She wondered if the water for the baths came from the lake or some other source. They skirted around the Hall of Elements before approaching the front of the bathhouse building.

The entrance to the bathhouse was impressive in its way. Not as large as the Hall of Elements, not by half, it sported a broad marble staircase fronted by columns that supported an archway over wide double doors. Anise stopped to admire the columns. Maeve marched confidently up the stairs, followed by her ducklings.

"Come on, Anise," called out Jord.

Anise was a little uncomfortable at first getting undressed in the bathhouse. Maeve explained that there were many different pools and rooms. Some were just for the masters, some were for students, and some were for women only. They went to one of the rooms that was for women only. After pointing out the room for them, Maeve went off on her own. Anise wasn't sure where to.

The pool they were lying in was in that room. Anise lay back between Cian and Jord, soaking in the deliciously warm water. The pool was exactly the right temperature. Somewhere between hot and warm. Just the perfect somewhere. Maeve had told her that students were assigned to practice their elemental talents by producing fire to heat rocks in the water and maintain the ideal temperature.

They were alone in the small stone-lined room, except for a few other women on the other side of the pool. The warm water flowed into the room through a channel at the bottom of one wall. The warm water flowed in one channel, and cooler water flowed out another.

She was relaxed now. The warm water and her companion's company had removed her doubts.

"You know what the Key is, don't you?" said Jord.

Anise met her eyes. Jord had a bit of a crooked smile on her face.

"Relaxing?" Anise asked.

"No," said Jord, "I mean the Key to alchemy."

Cian looked up. She looked first at Anise, then at Jord. She made a shushing gesture with one finger on her lips to Jord. Jord ignored her.

"Well," Jord continued, "You remember how a Key is a thing, a place, and an idea simultaneously?"

"Yes," said Anise, "Master Ernst gave us those little vials. The Key to Alchemy is the liquid in them."

Jord nodded. "That's the thing." She made a broad gesture that took in the walls of the room around them and the pool they were lying in. "The bathhouse is the place." She laughed. "Get the idea?"

Anise was confused. She turned her head toward Jord. "No," she said.

Cian looked down at the water they were soaking in. She had a melancholy expression on her face.

Jord laughed again. "I'm sure Master Ernst will talk about the mystical properties of bodily fluids. But, the reason that the academy bathhouse is the Place is that the masters-only baths have an outlet that leads to a room where they fill those little bottles. Apparently, the water the masters soak in is very potent."

Anise frowned. She looked searchingly at Jord with a shadow of distress on her face. "That's gross," she said.

4

Anise and Cian were both in the same clairvoyance class. Vin and Jord weren't in that class either. At first, Anise wasn't sure why. Cian and Anise still hadn't exchanged more than a few words, but the older girl had stopped shying away from Anise when she came close, so that was progress.

Anise guessed that Cian was a little older than her. Perhaps a year. She was shorter, though not anything like as small as Maeve. She had her mother's red hair and brilliant green eyes, though it was hard to see them as she avoided eye contact.

After noticing Anise looking back and forth between her and Cian, Maeve had commented one time, "Remind me to tell you about the birth sometime." Then she laughed and continued, "Or better, don't."

The clairvoyance class was in an undistinguished building on the edge of campus. The master was a middle-aged woman, though, to Anise, she seemed unutterably old. She was exceptionally unexceptional, dressed in her black master's robes with her straight brown hair hanging just to her shoulders.

"Now," she said, "those of you who are expecting to be able to forecast the future after your first class with me, I am afraid I have to disappoint you. This class is going to be more theoretical than practical." She looked down at her notes. "We're going to be doing a lot of reading."

Anise thought that perhaps she knew why Vin and Jord hadn't been assigned to the class.

"Clairvoyance is a lost art," continued the master. Anise read the slate behind the podium. "Master Huginn" was written there. "A long time ago, it was one of the disciplines here."

The master frowned and looked down at her notes again. "It's unclear what happened, but within a short period, two hundred years ago, the Academy curriculum went from having five disciplines to having just four."

Master Huginn shuffled her papers. "I am a researcher here at the Academy. When Master Lorenzo approached the Academy council with his proposal that the study of clairvoyance should be re-added to the curriculum, he encountered skepticism."

Master Huginn shook her head. "I'm giving you too much politics," she said. "Let me start again."

Anise thought she could see why the master was a researcher rather than a lecturer.

Master Huginn lifted her head from her notes and looked out at the class. "That same two hundred years ago, the Academy library was intentionally stripped of books on, and references to, the discipline of clairvoyance. Finding that shocked me as a researcher. It brought me firmly to the opinion that Master Lorenzo was right. We need to bring clairvoyance back to this school."

The master shook her head again as if she was still having trouble deciding what information she should be giving the class.

"This class is an experiment," she said. "We don't know how to teach clairvoyance. We have no books, no method, and no equipment. We're starting with first-years, as you won't have any preconceptions about what is or isn't possible. Your assignments will be finding and researching references to clairvoyance in the library. You will be helping the Academy regain lost knowledge."

The master pointed to the door in the back of the room. "Anyone who isn't interested in this curriculum is welcome to drop the class. Just speak to the registrar."

Master Huginn lifted a paper. "This is a list of books in the library that still contain some reference to clairvoyance.

Your first assignment will be to go to the library and locate and familiarize yourself with one of the books on this list.

"Even though the registrar's process puts those with gaps in their education into an appropriate class, sometimes people who have trouble reading slip through the cracks. Please familiarize yourself with the library's reading alcoves if you have trouble reading. The reading aids from last year had overstayed their welcome. I believe Master Lorenzo channeled a new set just last weekend, so there should be a fresh reading aid in each alcove."

5

Anise stepped up onto the stairs at the front of the library building. Marble columns supported a triangular pediment above the entrance. There were four alcoves, each containing a black stone gargoyle, in the pediment. They all glared down at Anise as she started climbing.

She hesitated at the top of the stairs. A shimmering transparent glow hovered across the wide-open double doors leading into the library interior. A friendly-looking young man was seated behind a high counter in the entrance hallway just beyond the glow.

"Can I help you?" he called out to Anise as she stood there.

Anise braced herself and stepped through the glow and up to the desk, trying to seem confident and unafraid. She felt a bit of a tingle as the glimmer surrounded her, but nothing else happened.

"I'm looking for a friend," she said to the young man. "She said she was going to be in a reading alcove."

The young man smiled at her and pointed to an opening on the right-hand side of the entrance hall. The words 'Reading rooms' were written on a sign over the archway.

Beyond the doorway was a corridor that went on a long way. Both sides were lined with cubicles. Each alcove contained two chairs, a desk, a lantern, and a cage hanging over the back of the desk.

Anise looked into the nearby cubicles. Several of them had people sitting at the cubicle's desks. They each seemed to be listening intently to something, but the corridor was as silent as the grave.

Relieved that she wasn't going to have to spend a lot of

time hunting down the corridor of alcoves, Anise spotted the back of Jord's head in one of the nearer nooks.

As soon as she crossed from the corridor into the alcove's entry, Anise heard a low, raspy voice. It was reciting something. Jord turned as she noticed Anise.

"Anise," she called out. They had just seen each other that morning, but Jord still sounded excited. The raspy voice stopped immediately.

Anise looked around for Jord's books. There was nothing on the desk. The cage behind the desk had a built-in book rack made of the same metal as the enclosure's bars. A book was resting on the shelf. Anise moved closer to see a shape in the cage more clearly.

A bit bigger than a large cat, a small gray creature crouched in the enclosure. It stood on its hind legs, forelimbs held in front of it. The forelimbs ended in sharp-looking claws of black material hard as stone. It had a round head with two small horns of the same black substance. Leathery dark gray wings flapped idly behind its back. Crinkled skin textured between rough leather and tree bark covered the creature's body. It had a tail with the same leathery texture. The appendage wrapped prehensily around its legs.

As Anise stepped nearer to the desk where Jord was sitting, the creature turned to look at her. If it hadn't been for the expression of singleness of purpose and focus on its face, the face might have seemed almost childlike and human.

She shuddered and stopped. "What's that?" she asked nervously.

Jord smiled. "That's my reading aid," she said cheerfully. "I call him Iggy." The creature turned its gaze toward her as she spoke. "Iggy, say hi to Anise," she said.

The creature turned back to Anise. "Burn," it said in the same low, raspy voice Anise had heard when she stepped into the alcove.

"Doesn't Iggy have a sexy voice?" said Jord.

"Uh-huh," said Anise carefully. "He has a name?"

"I think he's a fire imp," said Jord. "I don't know if he has a name. I just started calling him that. Let me show you how it works," she continued enthusiastically. "Iggy, read page three."

There was a faint rustling noise, and some of the pages in the open book turned over by themselves. The raspy voice resumed. Anise thought she heard a smoky quality in the sound that she hadn't noticed before. It was talking about potions, ingredients, and volumes of liquids.

"Is that our alchemy textbook?" said Anise.

"Iggy, stop," said Jord. The voice stopped immediately. Jord continued, "Yes, it is. Iggy's not much of a conversationalist, but he reads a treat. I tried talking to him, but it didn't work too well. Iggy, tell Anise about your interests."

The creature turned toward Anise. A wistful expression crossed its face. Anise tried to determine if she saw innocence or an absence of understanding in that expression.

"Burn?" said Iggy hopefully.

6

The second class in alchemy convinced Anise that Master Ernst wasn't only the oldest human being she had ever seen; he was also the dullest. The master droned on through the first half of the class. Somehow he managed to make the fact that one of the ingredients in their potions was used bathwater, dull, in addition to being disgusting.

"The Key to alchemy is the concept that the fluids of the human body hold power," said the master. His high, reedy voice pierced through to all the classroom seats, but the shrill sound sucked the life out of his words.

"Of course, there are other ingredients in alchemical potions," the master continued, "but a classic recipe will always contain some essence of liquid from a person."

Master Ernst lifted his eyes and gazed out over the students. His piercing gaze cut right into Anise as it passed over her. His eyes were a bright blue, though they were fogged just a bit by cataracts.

"Sometimes from the potion brewer. Sometimes a drop from the Key," he held up a small pink crystal vial, similar to the ones passed out to each student before class. "Sometimes, a potion calls for some bodily fluid from the person who is to be targeted by it.

"An elixir of mind control, for example, is more effective (some would argue only effective) if it contains a drop of blood from the person who is to be controlled."

The master frowned as he continued, "There are those, in these debased times, who argue that potions can be brewed without employing bodily fluids."

He concluded dramatically. "Until you show me a tincture of terror that manages to frighten a mouse without a drop of human spit in it, my faith will not be shaken."

Jord turned to Anise and whispered quietly, "Do you think when he was young, he bored the other Romans as much as he's boring us now?"

7

Anise and Jord were sitting in the reading alcove in the library again. This alcove had become Jord's favorite spot to study. Iggy watched the two of them from the safety of his iron-barred cage. Anise had gotten used to the intensity of his gaze.

"Why weren't you at our first channeling class?" said Jord. "I thought you came here planning to study channeling."

"Did you have a dream telling you where it was?" asked Anise.

"I did," said Jord. She smiled proudly. "Vin heard that they did something to make it more likely that students with channeling ability would have those dreams. She didn't have one herself." Jord's smile drifted a little toward self-satisfaction. "She asked me where it was, but I wouldn't tell her."

Iggy stuck one of his obsidian claws between the iron bars of his cage. He focused on Jord with a yearning expression on his face and said, "Burn?"

"No, of course, you can't burn her," said Jord to the imp. "I don't know what you're thinking." She frowned at the fire imp. "Sometimes, Iggy," she said. She stopped and looked thoughtful, "Anyway, she likes fire."

"What was the dream like?" asked Anise. She was genuinely curious, as she wanted to compare it to her own.

"Dreamy," said Jord. "It was like I woke up in the way-house dorm, but all the bunks except mine were gone. No one else was there. Vin's bed was empty. I don't know where you were."

Jord looked thoughtful. "I've never had a dream like that before. It felt both more and less real than my usual dreams." She hesitated, then continued. "More real, in that it felt powerful, like things were really happening. Less real in that I knew that I was dreaming."

Jord took a breath and leaned toward Anise excitedly. "There was a spirit there, a Daemon. She was beautiful, though her skin was green. She said her name was Fyki, and she was there to help me." Jord looked confused. "She said she was the spirit of kelp or something like that. She told me where the class was going to be."

Anise looked away from Jord. Her gaze crossed Iggy's. He seemed to be staring at her. His pupils were fully dilated like a cat's in a dark room. Anise dropped her gaze to the ground.

"Did it feel like someone was watching you?" she said carefully.

Jord looked surprised. "No, I told you there was no one there in the room but me and the Daemon." She shook her head, "Who would have been watching me?"

Anise looked thoughtfully at the ground, remembering Helios's warning that she should keep a low profile. She didn't reply.

Jord looked sternly at Anise. "Promise me that you won't miss the next class," she said. "I don't want to have to go alone again."

"Wouldn't dream of it," said Anise.

8

Anise and Cian walked together to illusion class. When Anise had suggested that they walk together, Cian favored her with a shy smile. The smile, and a pair of bright green eyes, glowing like emeralds, peeked out at Anise from under an unruly mop of red hair. Anise took the smile as assent, and they made their way to the classroom together in companionable silence.

Anise and Cian found seats toward the back of the classroom. Master Devona stepped up to the podium.

One of the students in the front row held up a hand. The master acknowledged him with a nod.

"Master Devona," he said, "They've been talking about the Keys to the disciplines in our other classes. Could you tell us about the Key to illusion?"

"I guess you've heard something about Keys," she said. "Otherwise, you wouldn't be asking the question." She looked around the class, seemingly trying to meet each student's gaze one by one. "Well, as you know, the Key to a magical discipline is, at one and the same time, a place, an idea, and a thing.

"I won't talk about the place and idea of the Key to illusion just yet, but the thing that is Key to Illusion is the absence of a thing that is Key to Illusion. The physical Key to the discipline of illusion is that there is no physical Key."

9

Anise spent an uncomfortable amount of time at meals at the way-house looking at Niall. She tried to be careful. She tried to avoid looking when anyone else might see, but he was just so pretty. He was tall, like her uncle, and had straight brown hair that might feel soft and warm to the touch, like a loaf of bread fresh out of the oven.

She was careful to make sure that no one saw her looking, especially Jord and Vin. Jord would tease her in a friendly way if she knew. Vin's teasing would probably not be so kind.

One time Anise thought she saw Maeve noticing her looking. She just smiled at Anise and passed the peas.

The cook's boy, Raphael, served food to the table before he sat down to join the group and eat himself. Several times, Anise found her view of Niall interrupted by Raphael putting something on the table or asking her if she needed something. A slight boy, Raphael was probably not much younger than Anise but seemed younger due to his size. He had red hair. His hair color made her think of Rufus from the Caravan of Wonders.

Anise hadn't spoken much to Niall. He was an upperclassman, and she worried he wouldn't have time for a first-year like herself. Vin seemed comfortable chatting away with him. Anise found herself envious when Vin sat next to Niall at mealtimes.

10

J ord and Anise barely had time to sit down in elements class before Master Videmon bid all the students rise. The master smiled. "We're going on a field trip today," he said. Seeing some of the class looking around them to grab their books and bags, he continued, "Don't worry, it's not a very long trip." The master pulled a bulky ornate key from his belt and approached the solid metal door on the narrow classroom's inner wall.

The key was large, crafted of metal, like the polished door, and was painted in forceful colors. Anise saw red, brown, blue, and white bands around the shaft. Master Videmon handled it reverently.

The master unlocked the door and swung it open; it swung open silently. Master Videmon stood beside the open door and gestured to the interior.

"This way, please," he said amiably. The students started filing through the door.

When it was Anise's turn to step past the master and into the corridor on the other side, she had to overcome a moment of claustrophobia. The passageway on the other side of the metal door was not much broader than the doorway itself. It was low, dark, and led straight as an arrow into the blackness away from the classroom.

Master Videmon stepped into the corridor after the last of the students, turned behind himself, swung the heavy door closed, and locked it. The darkness and stillness were absolute. Anise felt she couldn't breathe.

A light appeared through the darkness. Master Videmon held up his hand, and a glowing sphere appeared above it. Anise examined the sphere curiously. She was close enough that she would have felt the heat from a ball of fire, and this globe didn't feel warm. It also was more yellow and white than red. For an instant, she wondered if it could be that light was its own element and if there might be more than four elements.

Then Master Videmon set off down the corridor, gesturing for the class to follow him. Such heretical thoughts were driven from her head.

They reached a staircase after a shuffle along the narrow corridor. It was probably shorter than it felt. The flights of stairs wound down for a long time. It was hard to judge both time and distance in the dim space.

The stairs ended, and after another short corridor, they approached another door-a twin to the one from the classroom. The master opened this one with the key as well. He repeated his gesture of standing by the door and letting the class file by him. All Anise could see was a red glow coming through the doorway.

As Anise, the last of the students, walked by the master, he called out in a theatrically loud voice, "Welcome to the Key to the discipline of the Elements!"

Anise milled through the group of her fellow students and wasn't able to see much. The floor of the space beyond the door was cobbled stone. Anise was a little confused. Had they come back outside? Everything looked red, and the air felt warm.

Anise reached the edge of the group of students and the cobbled area, grasped a stone railing, and looked up.

Her mouth dropped open. The space above and before her felt as vast as the outside. Everything was suffused with a red glow, but it was the source of that glow that loosened her jaw. Below the railing she held, and her grip on the stone tightened as she looked, was a drop to a body of water wide enough to be called a river. Beyond that was a mountain of rough black stone rising to an open peak flowing red with lava streams. The whole thing was contained within the building. The far walls were visible at the limits of Anise's vision (though the smoke and steam from the water and heat reduced that limit).

There was a spiraling vortex of clouds around the peak of the mountain. Below the clouds, the top of the stone summit was open in a fuming crater. Anise felt she could barely make out the ceiling high above the spire and the clouds. There was a hint of an opening in the roof. A trace of blue sky peeked in just over the volcano's crater. The spiraling winds funneled and conveyed the smoke and fumes through the hole.

"It's a small volcano," said Master Videmon to the group, "as such things usually go." He spoke forcefully to be heard over the rumble of the distant lava and the murmuring bluster of the winds.

"Of course," continued the master, "Volcanoes inside buildings isn't how such things usually go." The master laughed. If he hadn't amused any of his students, at least he had amused himself.

Master Videmon lifted both arms above his head. "Do you feel it, my students?" he said. "Do you feel the power, the elements?"

Anise did. There was a strong odor of sulfur in the air. She felt the hot wind on her face and the swirling mist rising from the distant river below. They filled her with a feeling of strength. She felt that capturing and controlling these elements would be easy to learn.

"Of course," said Videmon, laughing again. He was amusing himself today. "If you don't feel it here, you're probably in the wrong class."

THE ISLE OF THE WISE

1

Their channeling class was in a stone building on the lakefront. Since coming to Ashton and the Academy, Anise hadn't been down to the lake. Jord made her lead the way, as she wanted to be very careful to make sure she wasn't being tricked into giving away where the class was being held.

"If I wouldn't tell my sister, who I have trouble hiding things from," she said, "I don't think I should be telling you."

Helios had told Anise where to go, so she didn't have a problem.

It was late afternoon. As Anise and Jord walked through the Academy toward the class, the afternoon sun was cut off by a forceful mist that reached out from the lake. The entrance to the classroom was on the side of the building. Some wharves stretched out into the water from the structure's lakeward face.

The wharves were shrouded in the mist. Anise thought she saw several large rowboats tied up by the docks.

The classroom was similar to the rooms for Anise's other classes. The now-familiar black slate was behind the master's podium. The master wasn't there yet; Cian was, however. She was sitting in the last row away from the master's desk. Behind the last row of seats were open windows looking out over the lake. Cian nodded to Anise and Jord when they sat down next to her.

A cold, clammy breeze was coming in through the windows behind them. Anise turned and looked out over the water and the wharves. The mist was thick enough that there wasn't much to be seen beyond the docks and the nearby waters. The quiet sound of gentle lake waves knocking the tied-up boats against the wood filled the air.

Anise turned back around. Jord and Cian were discussing something from the last class, perhaps. The master entered the classroom, and Anise shushed them.

The master stepped up to the podium. Anise noticed that Jord and Cian were looking at her, not the man in front of the class. She gasped as she looked at the master's face. Or perhaps, better said, at where his face should be. A massive scar ran diagonally across his face from his forehead's left-hand side, across the center, to the right-hand side of his chin. There was little left of his nose, and it left one not knowing where to look. Bright, intelligent brown eyes peered out through the ruin beneath a youthful-looking head of brown hair.

Jord reached out and touched Anise's hand. "Vin heard that it was a mountain reaver raid when he was a child. The raiders left him for dead, but he didn't die."

Anise had heard of the mountain reavers. A tribe of savages that supposedly lived in the Etenies just past the borders of Liamec in the northwest. She had thought them a myth.

"Welcome class; to our second session," said the master. "Or, for some of you, our first." His clear eyes scanned the classroom. Anise thought that they rested on her for a moment. The name Master Callum was written on the slate behind him. His voice was clear and vigorous, though there was a bit of a strange sound to it, which Anise attributed to the damage to his jaw and lips.

"As I mentioned in our last class," continued the master, "today we will begin some practical exercises." He opened a leather satchel and brought out several candles.

"If those of you sitting in the back could close the windows," the master said, "I'm going to try to lead you all through a controlled channeling session." He set the candles down on the desk in front of him and lit them. A sage-like scent started to fill the air. "Mugwort," he said with satisfaction.

"As I mentioned in our last class, a good part of this year will be dedicated to acquiring control. You need to control when you travel to dream and, perhaps more importantly: when you don't. If everyone could look next to your desks," the master continued, "you should find a rolled-up sleeping pad there. We're going to journey together to the realm of dreams." The master laughed, "It's nap time."

2

Anise opened her eyes and sat up. The classroom looked the same, though there were fewer desks, and she was the only one there. The familiar feeling of dream flooded into her. She stood and looked around. Was Helios coming to see her?

The door to the classroom opened, and a young man entered. Anise didn't feel that she had ever seen him before. Though he seemed familiar in the way you know someone in a dream.

She thought of Briac. She still thought of Briac on occasion, though the time they had shared on her journey to the Academy seemed like a lifetime ago.

She thought of Briac because she had thought Briac handsome. Next to this young man, her memories of the lines of Briac's hardy face felt like a fountain by a waterfall. His face shone in her dream, like Helios's, though with beauty rather than light.

The young man walked over to her. His bright brown eyes captivated her. "Anise," he said. Anise waited for him to continue, a little lost.

"Seeing as you missed our first class," the man continued matter-of-factly, "I'll start with some basics."

"Master Callum?" said Anise.

The young man frowned. "Of course," he said.

"But your face?" Anise stammered. Then she blushed and turned her gaze to the ground.

The master gazed at her calmly. "Who would dream that they had a face like that?" he asked.

When Anise didn't reply, Master Callum continued, "Anyway, basics, as I said."

"How are you here, sir?" said Anise. "In my dream?"

"That's a bit beyond the basics," said Master Callum. He laughed. Anise watched with fascination as the laugh made his face friendlier and more handsome. "But we must encourage inquiry.

"I am what's called a dream-walker," said the master. "This is your dream, certainly, but at the same time, I am making it mine as well. I will be visiting the dreams of each of your classmates in turn. A bit of personalized instruction."

"How do you do that? Can I do that? Can any channeler do that? Can you do that, even if I don't want you to? Can you go anywhere you want in the dream world?"

The master laughed again. Anise felt like making him laugh was probably a goal she might want to strive for in and of itself.

"So many questions. Like I said, basics. First off, you are here and not off gibbering quietly to yourself in some madhouse somewhere because you know the answer to your last question instinctively." The master gestured around them at the classroom they were standing in. "This is what is called the 'circle of light.' Your channeling dreams always have a circle of light. A channeler summons forces, or creatures, into the 'circle of light' but doesn't leave it."

"I saw you come in through that door," said Anise.

"I'm sure it looked that way," the master replied. "I made your dream into a common dream with my own. If we were to open that door and look out, I don't know what we'd see. I know what would happen if we were to step out. Madness, and probably death. The lesson I stressed beyond all others in the first class, which you missed, was: never leave the circle of light. Here be dragons."

3

Anise was sitting next to Maeve at dinner. Maeve had her claimed spot at her selected table, and woe betide anyone who thought about sitting there. The other seats were available for anyone, and Anise sometimes sat next to Maeve.

Rafael stood behind Anise, holding a soup pot almost as big as he was. "Anise," he said, "do you want some soup?"

"Put that on the table, Raffy," said Anise. "You'll drop it." She moved to clear some space on the table next to her bowl.

"I can hold it," said Rafael. He huffed a bit as he moved the pot closer to the table's edge.

Anise reached for the ladle that was sticking out of the pot. She spooned some of the soup into her bowl. Rafael turned to Jord, who was sitting on the other side of Anise.

Anise looked around the table. She missed Oscar. He had talked about things that weren't about Ashton, the Academy, or the weather. He spoke of his travels, conditions in other parts of Liamec, and places and things he'd seen. He even talked about politics.

One of Oscar's frequent topics of conversation was how the prince regent, the young lion as he was called, was taxing the people of Liamec to excess.

"He's making the poor poorer and the rich richer," he had said. "It's wrong, and something needs to be done."

No one else really disagreed when Oscar talked like this. In fact, no one really replied. The affairs of the regent and the king's court in the distant King's Seat in the city of Capitol seemed very far away to them all. It didn't have much to do with the food on the table or what classes they had tomorrow.

Anise looked around again. Vin was quiet. Sometimes Anise got the impression that she didn't feel like any of them were worth talking to. Her new friends at the Academy were not the poor that Oscar had been defending. Anise thought she had seen Vin frowning at some of Oscar's comments.

Niall was carefully spooning his soup into his mouth. Anise studied his face like one might appreciate a work of art. There was something about his nose; it was a straight Greek nose. It gave his profile a strength that she found appealing.

Jord and Cian were talking loudly about something. Anise listened in. They were talking about something that Master Callum had said in channeling class. Cian had started talking to Anise and Jord now. In fact, sometimes, it was hard to get her to stop talking.

Maeve leaned over toward Anise. "A penny for your thoughts, my dear," she said.

"Maeve," said Anise. Tears started to well up in the corners of her eyes. "I would have been so homesick without you."

4

Master Ernst was slow and careful with the instruction of the alchemy class. Like his shuffling walk had implied he might be each time he approached his podium. Jord kept talking about how boring the master was. Still, Anise found the idea that he'd been here since the Academy's founding quite fascinating. She kept wondering about what he must have seen, what he must know about things at the Academy, and how they worked. The thought that a drop of his essence was in each potion the students made since he bathed at the bathhouse was also interesting in its own way.

For the first three classes, the master did nothing but talk. He spoke of the theory and practice of alchemy. What kind of flasks to use, how ingredients were prepared, and how they interacted with each other. He tried to instill some feeling of the science's greater purpose and responsibility. Reagents, reasons, and retorts. Jord just wanted to make a potion that would turn someone into a frog. Not that she had anyone she wanted to turn into a frog, just as an academic exercise.

By the fourth class, they finally got to go to the lab. The lab was next door to the classroom. It was divided up into stations. The master instructed them to split up into teams, with each team taking a station. Jord and Anise immediately claimed one of the stations toward the middle of the room. Vin and her friend, who still usually wore purple, took one toward the back.

The station was a little raised counter area above the floor. There was a sink, a bucket with clean water, and a set of glass tubes, vials, and retorts. Anise had never seen so much glass in one place at the same time before. Glass was expensive and, therefore, a bit uncommon.

The walls were lined with cabinets and shelves filled with exotic plants and jars containing strange substances. Anise quickly gave up trying to make sense of the bewildering array of smells that assailed her nose.

The master made an announcement from the front of the room. He was trying to look stern, but the effect was spoiled when his voice broke partway through and became even more reedy and high-pitched. "Be careful with the glass," he said, "whatever pieces you break will be taken out of your hides." After that warning, he described the morning's assignment in excruciating detail.

Brewing the potion was easy. Anise was relieved when she and Jord finished the assignment without a problem. It made her feel good when Master Ernst praised their work. He held up the vial they had produced, examined the liquid through the light, and sniffed it. He said, "Excellent work, you two. This has a fine bouquet," he paused and took a delicate sip of the brew, "and an excellent body."

He picked up a seedling in a small pot from the central table. "Now, for the real test," he said. The master poured about half the liquid in the vial into the earth around the small plant. There was an audible crackling sound as the sprout shot up to twice its height in a flash. The ceramic side of the pot cracked, and a small root thrust its way out into the open air.

"Well done," said Master Ernst with a smile.

5

Anise woke up. She sat up in her bunk bed. The feeling of being in a dream washed over her. Her bed was alone in the dorm room again. Her forehead felt flushed as if there was some light or warmth in the air. Her first thought was that Helios was visiting her in the dream realm again.

She recognized the circle of light that Master Callum had spoken of. The room was lit by simple candlelight, but it felt like a friendly ring of warmth and safety. She shivered when she tried to imagine what was outside the wooden walls. She realized now that she had always known to stay in the circle, though until the master had said it, she hadn't been conscious of her knowledge.

It wasn't Helios. Iggy was hovering in the air just a few feet from her bunk. His little leathery wings, flapping fiercely to keep him immobile, stretched and gloried in the freedom of flight. The warmth seemed to be coming from him.

"Iggy," said Anise. "What are you doing here?"

Iggy's catlike eyes pondered her. His face, hard to read at the best of times, seemed to be showing a quizzical expression as he said, "Burn?"

All at once, Anise knew why Iggy was there; she had summoned him. She hadn't done it consciously. Her thoughts and speculations had been of Iggy, channeling, and the world of dreams. She was disappointed in herself and knew that Master Callum would also be disappointed in her. He had talked about focusing on control and discipline.

Anise felt a surge of panic. She was in a channeling dream, without Helios to hide her from the watcher. Then she realized that she didn't feel the watcher's presence. *It makes sense*, she thought. *He can't watch all the time.*

Anise stood up and stepped toward Iggy. She wasn't afraid of him. For one thing, she didn't feel a sense of menace, and for another, she thought he knew that she had been the one who had gotten him out of his cage, though she had no idea how that had happened.

"Do you want to go back, Iggy?" she asked.

Iggy fixed his gaze on her. His pupils had gotten even wider in the dim candlelight; His eyes looked almost wholly black. "Burn!" he said defiantly, shaking his head.

Iggy turned from Anise and flew rapidly over toward the outside wall of the dorm room. He briefly paused in front of the wall, then sped directly toward the wood. There was a crashing sound, and a cloud of smoke and steam obscured the area.

"Iggy!" called out Anise as she ran after him. She reached the wall as the smoke and steam faded. There was an Iggy-shaped hole in the wood of the wall. The edges were smoldering, though the wood looked thin and hazy. Anise considered looking through the hole. Then she shivered and thought better of it. Iggy was gone.

6

Anise didn't take to illusion. At least not the big impressive illusions Master Devona demonstrated for the class and that her fellow students were eager to emulate. She wasn't sure she wanted to make an illusionary dragon soar through the sky or conjure an insubstantial castle from mist and cobwebs.

"They're not really there, are they," she complained to the master as the class worked on conjuring an image of a coin as an exercise. "It's like lying."

"I suppose that's true," said Master Devona thoughtfully. Then she laughed and lifted her hands into the air. Shining gold coins dropped from her fingertips and vanished after hitting the floor with a distinctive sound. Anise had never heard it before, but she still recognized the thud of a heavy piece of gold hitting a hard surface. "But, I'm not sure I care," continued the master. The bright shining gold disks falling from her hands were like the ringlets in her hair.

Master Devona continued. "If you remember, the physical key to illusion is that there is no physical key to illusion." Her smile warmed Anise.

Anise couldn't help it, but whenever she saw Master Devona, she never failed to remember a poppet that her mother had made for her. It had yellow yarn for hair and a permanent smile on its cloth face. It made her sad to remember her mother.

"And the targeted ones," said Anise sadly, "They're worse. You don't even get to control what they look like. That's up to the target."

Master Devona smiled again, or perhaps still. "I'm not sure they would say that it's up to them. They don't have a conscious choice about what appears. It's a weave between the desires of the illusionist and the target's mind. They often don't appreciate the image."

"Still," said Anise stubbornly, "If that's what illusion is, I don't like it."

Master Devona looked serious. The change of expression made her look even more doll-like and charming. Like when your dog tilts his head to look at you as if he was trying to understand the secret mysteries of the universe.

"Well, Anise," she said, "though we usually emphasize two forms of illusion: display and targeted, there is a third."

Anise waited patiently for the master to continue.

"Transformative. Most people prefer the flashier ones. Transformative illusion is the illusionary transformation of a thing that really exists into another form of itself. Making a bridge appear to have collapsed or hiding a doorway or gap in a wall. It's useful for hiding, traps, and changing one's appearance. It's sometimes called glamour. I have to confess, I'm a little older than I look." The master's smile grew a little rueful with this last comment.

Anise almost laughed with relief. "I like that," she said. "That's what I'll do."

7

Anise had gotten quite tired of digging through old books in the library for her clairvoyance class. There was usually just one small reference to clairvoyance or the teaching of clairvoyance. Master Huginn greeted each discovery with an excitement that was contagious, however. She would smile and light up. It made her look a little less unexceptional.

Anise was sitting in what had been Iggy's reading alcove. He had been replaced with a water imp. She was trying to ignore the sad look on the imp's face. There was a bit of a sloshing noise when he moved around in his enclosure. The bottom of the pen had a waterproof lining and was filled with a murky liquid. Anise hoped it was water. The imp had bluish moist-looking skin with a texture that reminded Anise of fish scales.

She had taken to thinking of him as Drippy. Anise had been unable to get him to say anything except while reading. There was a small pile of books on the desk, and one was open in the book slot beside the imp's enclosure.

Drippy was reading to her from the book. Anise was tired and had thought that having Drippy read the book would be less tiring than reading it herself. She wasn't sure that it had been a good idea. Drippy's voice was smooth and rhythmic, like water flowing over river rocks. It had a certain wet quality to it. She started to think of it as a squishy voice. It was putting her to sleep.

Anise dozed off briefly, then woke with a start. She had a momentary vision of a bonfire. Why had she been dreaming of a bonfire? Drippy had stopped talking. Anise looked up toward his enclosure.

Iggy was hovering outside the enclosure, his wings flapping busily. Drippy was crouched on the bottom of the cage, looking up at the fire imp. After glaring momentarily at Drippy, Iggy peered at Anise, his black pupils feeling like they burned through her. He pointed the tip of his prehensile tail at the book that Drippy had been reading. He said, conversationally, "Burn."

Anise sat up and looked from side to side. "Iggy?" she said. "How did you get in here?"

Iggy picked up the book Drippy had been reading in his scaled claws, brought it over to her, and dropped it open on the desk. "Burn," he said forcefully.

Drippy watched Iggy. Anise wondered if there was a hierarchy in the imp world. It seemed Drippy was deferring to Iggy, though that may have had to do with who was in the cage and who was outside it.

She inspected the book. It was a journal from one of the masters at the Academy from a long time ago. The master's personal book collections were usually donated to the Academy library upon their passing. She scanned the open section. It was a report of a book burning. The master whose journal it was described stumbling across a group of fire imps burning a pile of books. *I'll have to take this to Master Huginn,* thought Anise. "Iggy?" she asked.

"Burn," said Iggy affirmatively.

8

Vin and Jord respectively took to elements class like a phoenix and a mermaid to fire and water. At their first class, Vin was already able to produce a burst of flame from her hand. Still, after Master Videmon showed her some techniques, she achieved a measure of power and control by the third class that he said rivaled some Academy graduates. Jord's mastery of the element of water wasn't far behind.

Anise didn't have such an easy time of it. She was able to get a feel for the elements of air, water, and earth. She could make the little fan on the lab counter spin with gusts of air. She could make water flow through the piping and tubes into the sink provided for the purpose. She could even make the steel spheres the master supplied them with clatter and clank together. But, no matter what she did, she couldn't produce a flame. When she snapped her fingers together in one of the gestures Master Videmon taught them, she was lucky if her fingertips felt a little warm.

The lab was in the Hall of Elements, like their classroom. As they worked at their lab station, Anise could feel the presence of the Key, the volcano, through the stone wall on the inside of the narrow, long chamber. The elemental forces flowed through the ether, through the wall, into her, and into the power she was summoning. Until she tried to conjure fire. She could feel the flames, but something was blocking them from flowing through her.

"Of primary concern," said Master Videmon, "is the source of the potential you draw from. Near the Key, the volcano and its effects will help you. It's the biggest and strongest power source near here, so it will be hard to draw from anywhere else."

Videmon showed particular interest in Jord and Vin's

progress in class. He praised them for their work and native aptitude. Anise remembered what Maeve had said about his interest in twins and wondered what his theories were.

"If you're summoning forces in a place where the wellspring of the element is not so obvious, you need to choose it, rather than just drawing on the nearest source." Videmon shook his head. "The nearest source is probably your own body."

Videmon clicked his tongue. "We've had students lose fingers from frostbite after sucking all the heat out of their bodies with a flame blast. Desiccation with water. Pulling the moisture from the air is harder but won't leave you in the infirmary."

9

Master Callum was excited. "We'll be having an adventure this afternoon," he said. He instructed the class to stand, form into lines, and follow him out of the classroom. The perpetual mist that shrouded the docks made it a little chilly as they all trouped out through a door they hadn't used before that led directly onto the docks.

"The first time is always the most interesting," said Master Callum. He had half the class sit in the first of two long oared boats tied up by the wharf. He instructed the rest to sit in the second. "Anise," he said, "Why don't you sit in the front of the second boat."

The master looked up, standing on the dock, and called out to all the students at once. "The Isle of the Wise is the Key to channeling. We will be making a trip to the heart of dreaming."

He untied the boats and lashed them together. He told the students in the first boat to take the oars. The second would just be towed. The master lit lanterns in the front of each rowboat, then took up a position in the stern of the first boat, his hand on the tiller.

Anise went and sat in the front seat of the second boat. Jord sat beside her. The light from the lantern cut through the mist, forming a circle of visible space around them. Anise smelled the now familiar smell of mugwort. The oil in the lamp must be mugwort infused, she thought.

Master Callum turned to Anise from the stern of the front boat. Anise had almost gotten used to seeing his ruin of a face, though seeing it over the lantern light, through the mist, was still startling. "Try to make sure the rope stays tied," he said. It was hard to see if he was smiling or not. "Sometimes, the second boat doesn't come back."

Jord gasped.

"I'm kidding," the master continued, "It usually comes back, eventually." The master used his steering oar to push off from the dock. The first boat drifted slowly away from the wharf. The second, pulled by the attached line, followed.

"Oars in the water," called out the master. "Row, my neophyte dreamers, row!"

Many of the students had never been in a boat before. There was a clattering and clunking sound as they tried to figure out how to use their oars. The sound echoed through the fog and disturbed the stillness of the misty waters.

Eventually, they formed some semblance of order and moved off into the mist. Master Callum used the tiller to guide the boats straight away from the dock toward the lake's center.

Anise tried to think inconsequential thoughts to conceal herself from the watcher. If this boat trip had something to do with channeling, he would be keeping an eye on them.

She watched the dock vanish into the mist with a shiver.

10

Anise walked along a gravel pathway. The gravel crunched beneath her feet with a satisfying sound. There was nothing to be seen except a thick mist around her. She felt like she was following a path through a grove of trees, but the thick fog obscured everything except the trail.

Anise thought she was walking alone, then she realized, with a start, that Master Callum was walking beside her.

"Master Callum?" she said. "Where are we? Where are the boats? Where's Jord?" She took him in more carefully. "What happened to your face?" The master was again the youthful, handsome young man she had seen in her first channeling class dream.

The master smiled and laughed. Anise was a little worried that he was laughing at her, then the infectious sound touched her, and she smiled back.

"Anise," Master Callum said, "Welcome to the Isle of the Wise, the Key to channeling." He flourished his arm in a gesture that would have been much more effective if there was anything to see but mist.

"Did we dock?" asked Anise.

The master's smile grew a little thoughtful. "You think it's a simple question, but it's really rather existential," he said.

Anise was a little annoyed. "Why won't you ever give me straight answers," she complained.

"Ask me some more questions, Anise," said the master, "I promise to answer them as straight as I can. That's what we're here for, after all."

"Who's the Watcher? What did you mean by 'Here be dragons.'? How do I get to be a dream-walker? How come I can sometimes channel a bit while awake?"

"All right," said the master. He lost his smile. "There's a lot to unpack there." He looked down at the gravel beneath their feet, then looked up and met Anise's eyes. His good looks took her breath away.

"I'll answer the easy one first. You can't channel while awake. That's not something that's ever been done, and I don't believe it ever will be." He frowned. "Then, moving on, I'll return with my own question. What do you mean by 'The Watcher.'?"

It was Anise's turn to look down at the gravel beneath their feet. "The Watcher," she said. "The man who watches our dreams here at the Academy." She wasn't comfortable mentioning that she had felt the Watcher in her dreams before coming to the Academy.

Master Callum looked relieved. "Oh, that's just Master Lorenzo." He smiled again. "He's just concerned for the students. As the head of the department here, he tries to keep track of the channeling to protect and safeguard the student body. You wouldn't believe what damage a bunch of untrained out-of-control young channelers can do. I suppose it's a form of dream-walking, what he does." As he said this last sentence, his expression changed to a more contemplative one.

"That's not it," said Anise. "The Watcher is looking for someone. He wants something. He's scared, and he's mean." She pointed to a spot in the mist-obscured sky as if the Watcher was behind the fog.

"I assure you," said Master Callum earnestly. "Master Lorenzo has the best interests of both the Academy and Liamec at heart. If he's watching us, it's for our protection and safety."

"How about 'Here be dragons'?" said Anise.

"Well," said Master Callum, "That's just a thing you say, isn't it? Here be dragons. It just means that there are monsters and dangers beyond the edge of the map. It's just to make you scared to even think about leaving the circle of light."

The master hesitated. "Though," he said, "There are old stories. People used to think that dragons lived both in this world and in another. That the world outside the circle of light is more than just death and insanity. They even say that people used to know how to travel there. Not just hop from one person's dream to another's, like I can, but explore outside the circle. They say that's where the truth lies." Master Callum shook his head as if shaking off a bad dream. "But, no one's seen a dragon in hundreds of years, and I sincerely advise you, Anise, not ever to leave the circle of light."

A few days later, in her next alchemy class, Anise asked Master Ernst about the Isle of the Wise. She figured that if he was older than the Academy, he must know if there really was an island out in the lake or if the mist was just a portal to the world of dreams.

"That's channeling stuff," said the master in his creaky old voice, "I don't bother with that. They all sniff too much mugwort if you ask me."

THE HALL OF THE HOLLY KING

1

The post came to the way-house once a week. There was usually something for Maeve. It was a big event whenever anyone else got a letter or a package. The rest of the residents of the way-house would crowd around asking what it was or who it was from.

When Anise took her letter from Aunt Rose back to her bunk and opened it alone, everyone was disappointed.

She started crying before she got through the greeting in the letter. Aunt Rose had addressed it to 'My darling Anise," and Anise felt her eyes begin to well up.

There wasn't much news in the letter. Things in the small town of Hero didn't change very fast or very often. Everyone in the village must have told Aunt Rose to send their love and greetings, and it seemed she had taken it literally. There were greetings from everyone Anise knew. Even some from villagers who she didn't really know that well.

Aunt Isabel shared something else with her greeting. "Tell Anise that we really miss her as a keeper for Twilight. No one else seems to be able to stop him from wandering off. Her Uncle Sebastian and I have spent hours hunting through the village for him."

There was a little news; of the small village sort. Uncle Sebastian and Aunt Isabel's farm was doing well. The crop was growing as it should, and the cows were content. Anise had one particular cow, who she called Buttercup. Sebastian and Isabel said that Buttercup's lowing was particularly plaintive because she missed Anise.

Anise started crying again as she reached the end of the letter. Uncle Sebastian wasn't coming to get her to take her home for the summer. It made sense, and through her tears, she understood, but the trip took too long. The time it took to travel from Ashton to Hero and back would take up most of the time that the Academy was out of session. Apparently, Lilith had already communicated with Maeve about Anise staying at the way-house over the summer.

It made sense, and Anise understood, but understanding comes in many forms. She was still crying when she put down the letter. Home felt very far away.

2

Anise's first year at the Academy rolled to a close. Jord and Cian were hesitant about the testing that the masters put the students through at the end of the school year, but Anise was confident in her abilities.

She passed her exams with flying colors. Master Devona was a little disappointed that she refused to embrace the more spectacular aspects of illusion. Still, her understanding of the concepts and her skillful application of transformative illusions put her in the ranks of the better students. Master Videmon assured her that her blockage with the element of fire would go away with time, and her grasp of the other elements was more than adequate.

Master Erst had taken a liking to Anise. As the master shuffled among the workstations watching the students work on the final assignment he had given them, he just nodded appreciatively when he saw Jord and Anise's work.

Master Callum was also pleased with Anise's progress. The primary focus of the first year of channeling training had been on learning how not to channel. Learning how to decide if a night's sleep would be broken by a channeling dream or not. In the last session, Master Callum told the class that Anise's ability to not channel was superior to any first-year student he had ever had.

Master Huginn from the clairvoyance class was happy with the progress that they had made as a group. "I will compile and study all the references you have found," she said. "Perhaps next year we will have a class where we actually try to learn something about the application of clairvoyance, instead of just trying to find out if it exists."

In some ways, Anise was worried about what the summer would bring. The break between academy sessions wasn't very long, as such things go, but it was long enough for her to wonder what she would do. The hot weeks of summer stretched in front of her like a desert.

The day when Vin, Jord, and Niall packed up and left the Way-house felt like an ending to her.

3

Maeve apologized to Anise about the way-house. "I'm afraid it will be boring this summer," she said. "It'll be just you, I, and Cian." She hesitated, "And, of course, Cookie and the cook's boy." She laughed. "I didn't mean to neglect them."

Anise shook her head. "Maeve," she said, "I am so grateful to you for letting me stay here."

Maeve looked thoughtful. "I hope you don't mind if Cian and I have some family things to do in the next few weeks." She paused before continuing, "we have some obligations we've neglected."

The following days were quiet. The Academy grounds were still open, and the guards would let Anise in. Still, no students wandered around campus, and most buildings were locked. Ashton itself was also quieter. Without the students occupying inns and guesthouses and traveling the streets, the town seemed a shadow of its former self.

One day Cian and Anise decided to go on an outing. They talked to the cook's boy, Raphael, about food for an excursion, and not only did he make it for them, but he also eagerly offered to help carry the basket. Anise looked skeptically at his skinny arms but couldn't find it in her heart to refuse.

As they walked through town to the park called the Dragon's Eye, Anise felt bad about the huffing and puffing coming from behind them, but Raphael refused any offers of help. He was following along behind her and Cian, still dressed in his cook's apron.

Anise wondered how Raphael could be so frail. As

Cookie's helper, he should be moving big things and working hard in the kitchen. Maybe Cookie took it easy on him and did the heavy stuff himself.

It got worse as they climbed the curving gravel path that spiraled around the hill up to the Dragon's Watchtower. Anise wished she had one of the potions they had brewed in her alchemy class. One session had been devoted to brewing a draught that refreshed the body and restored strength. If she'd had such a brew on her, she would have offered it to Raphael.

They reached the hilltop and found a spot to lay their blanket with a view of the town spread below them. Raphael stood gawkily beside the spread blanket until Anise insisted he sit and join them.

Raphael had packed an excellent meal. He sat awkwardly, cross-legged, on the edge of the blanket. Anise kept trying to get him to relax, join the conversation, or eat something. Still, he refused to soften, and he insisted that he had only packed enough food for her and Cian.

"So, Cian," said Anise, "what did your mother mean about family obligations?"

Cian looked leery as if trying to decide how much she could share. "My mother's family is," she paused, "complicated." She looked shyly down at the blanket, her coppery hair falling over her eyes.

"She made it sound like it would affect me," said Anise carefully.

"I think she was mostly thinking of the Litha," said Cian, "the solstice celebration." Cian looked up and met Anise's eyes. "You can hide in the dorm if you want, but it'll be hard to avoid it completely. The family can get a little rowdy."

Cian blinked, glanced over at Raphael, and continued, "We've been hosting it at the way-house for the last few years. Last summer, Cookie went home, and Raphael just hid in the dorm."

Raphael nodded, then looked down at the blanket himself, ashamed at his eruption of expression.

"The Litha?" said Anise.

"The battle between the Holly King and the Oak King," said Cian, as if that made it perfectly clear. "It's the day the days start getting shorter again, instead of longer. It's the longest day of the year. It's the day the sun goddess Sulevia spits on the solar usurper Helios. But, for my mother's family, it's mostly a chance to party."

It was Anise's turn to look down at the blanket. Partying hadn't been a big part of her life so far.

4

The days got longer. One day, that was almost as long as a day could be, Anise was sitting in the way-house common room. She was trying not to be affected by the heat. She was trying not to be affected by boredom. Her trying was interrupted by a knock on the door.

Anise jumped up. Visitors to the way-house had been few. She hoped for relief from the boredom. She opened the door.

She found herself face to face with a round ball of scarlet hair. So red, as to not look human, it was perched on the head of a man dressed in rough linen britches, without a tunic. His bare chest was covered in wiry, coppery hair and beautiful, colorful patterns, pictures, and images.

Anise had never seen a tattoo before, and she found herself fascinated by the colors, markings, and designs. Most of the tattoos were blue, but there were figures, lines, and parts of images in reds and yellows also.

The man had an iron link chain around his neck. It dangled down his bare chest. Anise wondered if the links ever caught in his chest hair. It was matched by a similar iron link belt that supported his britches. A wicked-looking sword hung from the belt on his left side.

The red ball on the top of his head was a bundle of braided hair. It was at Anise's eye level because the man was shorter than her. Just a little taller than Maeve, he was the smallest full-grown man Anise had ever seen.

Her eyes turned finally to his face. A big smile was spreading across the tanned features under a bristly mustache that matched the hair color of the bundle of hair atop his head. He started speaking. His voice was deep, melodic, and friendly, but Anise couldn't understand a word.

Anise turned and practically bolted for the corridor into the backrooms of the way-house. "Maeve!" she called out urgently.

Anise hid in the library. It was quiet there, and the massive stone building stayed cool inside, even on hot summer days. Maeve and Cian's family had been arriving for the evening's celebrations all day, and she didn't feel like she could help, so she wanted to stay out of the way.

The reading alcoves were a nice place to relax and be alone with her thoughts. Still, eventually, Drippy's forlorn expression got to be too much for her. Anise left the library and started on her way back to the way-house. As she walked through the tranquil Academy grounds, the late afternoon sun started considering whether or not it should begin its withdrawal from the sky.

Anise reached the now-familiar green building, number 13 Leafdrop Lane, and opened the door. Maeve locked up at night, but the door was never locked during the day. A man was standing just on the other side. Anise was startled. She had hoped to sneak through the common room and hide in her dorm room before the party started.

He was dressed, or not dressed, similarly to the man she had seen before. His upper body, bare from the waist, was covered with tattoos. Anise found her eyes caught again by the patterns and pictures.

He was startled, as well. He had been stationed or had stationed himself at the door as a greeter or guard. The door opening without a knock must have surprised him.

He recovered quickly. More quickly than Anise. He bowed deeply from the waist, then took her hand, looked up into her eyes, and said, "Welcome, my lady." He hesitated before continuing, "You must be the Lady Anise. Welcome to the hall of the Oak King." He spoke with an accent, as if English wasn't his first language, but clearly, and with a lilt in his voice that Anise found charming.

The small man stepped aside and swept his arm across

the common room with a welcoming gesture.

Anise gasped. The room had been transformed; she felt in another world. The walls had been covered with tree boughs, so none of the wall's wood showed through. The floor had been littered with flower petals. It felt more like a forest glade than a room in a house.

All the tables had been cleared from the open area, leaving a wide-open expanse crisscrossed by people. It was more people than she felt like she could count, certainly more people than she wanted to count. Everyone was dressed in various colors and fabrics, but the tattoos were a commonality. Anise was relieved to see that the women wore strips of cloth across their chests. Most of the men were bare-chested. The tattoos covered much of the exposed skin.

A stack of cut wood set up as a small bonfire was at one side of the room. Anise thought it was lit for a second, as it glowed as if burning. Then she saw that someone had arranged reflective surfaces in the windows that shone the setting sun's light into the room. Coming from multiple angles onto the woodpile, the orange and red glow of the setting sun was making Helios blush.

"Anise!" came a call from across the room. Cian charged across the floor to the door. Flower petals skittered away from her feet. She was taller than anyone in the room but Anise.

5

Cian grabbed Anise's arm and pulled her into the room. Cian was wearing an outfit like the rest of the women. She didn't have tattoos, but she wore a strip of cloth across her chest instead of a tunic. She pulled Anise over to the other side of the room. Anise looked down at the flower petals as they walked.

Two tables were set up there. One had a lavish spread of foodstuffs on it. Anise glanced at the dishes, but she had trouble recognizing what things were.

The other table was set up as a bar. Stools were lining one side of the table, piles of earthenware mugs on top, and several oaken casks were underneath. Maeve stood behind the table. She was also dressed like the other women in the room: colorful linen skirt and just a fabric bound around her chest in a matching pattern. Anise gaped a little as she regarded her housemistress. Maeve did have the colorful tattoos that the other people in the room wore. Anise realized that she hadn't seen Maeve without a full sleeve tunic before. When they had gone to the bathhouse, she had left to bathe in a different room.

"Close your talkbox," said Maeve. "You're gathering flies." She smiled to lessen the bite of her words. It seemed Maeve was tending bar. She put mugs in front of Cian and Anise and said, "What're you having?"

Anise just looked confused. Cian leaned over toward her and said, "There's mead and chouchen." She leaned even closer and whispered, "It's better if you drink chouchen. Some of them think of mead as a drink of the móra."

"What's chouchen?" asked Anise. "And móra?"

Maeve glanced at Cian. There was a bit of weight behind the glance, but Anise had no idea what it meant. "Well," Maeve said, "mead is honey wine. Chouchen is the nectar produced when you lead the work of nature's chosen insects, the bees, through the apple tree's fruit and into a blissful union with the sunlight of a glorious summer day. And móra? Well, you're móra, Anise." She smiled again.

"Oh," said Anise. "I guess I'll have some chouchen, then." She looked hesitantly over at the table with the enticing food and then at the amber fluid that Maeve was pouring into her mug. "I won't be in trouble if I eat this stuff, will I?"

"You mean, will you be trapped in faerie if you eat or drink the fae food?" Maeve laughed. "Look around, Anise. You know where we are. We're not in faerie; we're in my way-house. And, you're trapped here already, aren't you?"

Maeve slapped the mug down in front of Anise. It hit the wooden tabletop with a thud. It seemed to be something you did, as she did the same with the mug she put in front of Cian. Cian glanced sidelong at Anise and said, "Just take sips. There's bee's venom in the brewing, and it's strong."

Anise took a sip. The flavor was sweet but heady. It felt like she was taking a sip of a summer day. It was delicious.

"I was going to hide in the room," she said hesitantly to Cian.

"Too late, now," replied Cian.

A group of musicians had been tuning up in the corner, and they started playing. There was someone with a harp that was bigger than he was. There were two pipers and another person on a fiddle. The music was fast, tuneful, and infectious. Quickly many of the people in the room started dancing. The flower petals on the floor swirled around their feet.

A man walked over to Anise and Cian, sitting at the bar. Anise was about at his height, sitting on her chair, and their eyes met. It was the man she had opened the door to earlier.

"Anise," said Cian, "meet my uncle, Drest." She turned to the man standing before them and made an openhanded gesture toward Anise. "Uncle," she said, "meet Anise."

The man bowed, grasped her hand, and raised it to his lips. He said something in the same language he had used when she opened the door for him. There was a lyrical, musical quality to the sound, but she couldn't understand a word. Anise appealed to Cian for help with her eyes.

"He wants to know if you would like to dance," said Cian. She smiled. "Drest doesn't come to the móra towns much. He doesn't speak much English."

Drest started pulling on Anise's hand. He was surprisingly strong.

"I don't … I can't …" said Anise as she rose to her feet. The town of Hero had a weekly dance. It was held in the town square each Frigg's day evening. Anise had often gone with her friend Mary to watch the couples dancing. They hadn't danced themselves, however.

"Don't worry, you'll be fine," Cian called out to her as Drest pulled her out to where the couples were dancing.

6

The dances weren't that different from those she and Mary watched in the Hero town square. At first, Anise spent all her time looking at other people to see what they were doing and how they were moving, then she started to get the rhythm and began enjoying herself.

She warmed up. She had taken a second little sip of the chouchen in her mug before putting it down, and it left a pleasant feeling in her stomach. Drest smiled at her and encouraged her when she made a misstep in the dance. The other dancers gave her curious looks, but they also were very tolerant of her newness. She felt welcome.

Drest's iron chain and belt rattled as he moved. The sound was enough in rhythm with the dance that it sounded like part of the music.

The music stopped. One of the musicians produced a horn from somewhere and blew a blast on it. He tried to keep the sound down because he was indoors, but it was still distressingly loud. Drest walked Anise back over to the bar where Cian and Maeve were waiting, kissed her hand, and headed hurriedly down the hallway leading to Maeve's rooms.

"Where's he going?" asked Anise.

"You'll see," said Cian.

The dance floor cleared. The former dancers and those who hadn't taken part in the dancing formed a circle around the central space. The sun had set, and the reflected sunlight no longer lit the stack of wood. Some of the partygoers held lanterns. A dusky light cast shadows throughout the room. There were gaps in the circle of onlookers on both sides, one near the front door and the other near the corridor that led to Maeve's quarters.

A drumbeat started slowly, building steadily. It felt

like it was beating in time with Anise's heart. The crowd of people with their tattoos and strange clothing, the green leaves covering the walls, the dusky light, and the beating drum left Anise feeling like she had stepped into another world.

The door to the outside opened, and a man stepped in. He was dressed mainly like the rest of the crowd—bare-chested, tattooed, and with a sword strapped to his belt, but he wore a mask. He moved oddly as he stepped through the doorway and into the hall. He moved slowly, hesitantly. He moved how Anise might have imagined a tree would move if she had ever imagined a tree moving.

Two curled antlers rose out of the mask covering his whole head. The face was a grinning green visage of leaves and bark. It was expressive, that face; it gave a feeling of strength and life.

As the man in the mask moved slowly and with halting steps toward the middle of the room, the crowd started a low chant. It met and joined with the drumbeat, but the chant made Anise's heart feel like it was beating faster, whereas the drumbeat matched her heartbeat.

Cian leaned over and whispered in Anise's ear, "The Oak King. It's his hall now."

7

A horn blast blew. Similar to the horn blast that had halted the dancing but with a different tone. This sounded a call of warning. The Oak King lifted his head, his antlers raised toward what Anise knew must be the ceiling but felt like the night sky, and turned toward the sound.

The crowd, and Anise, turned to look where he was looking. Across the clearing, over the flower petals littering the wooden floor, down the hallway that led to Maeve's chambers. Slowly, carefully, another figure emerged from the shadows. Discreetly at first, but with increasing speed, a second man moved forward into the lamplight.

Anise thought she recognized the pattern of tattoos on the body of Cian's Uncle Drest, but this man moved similarly to the first. Hesitantly, and initially, slowly. He moved from the shadows into the circle of onlookers.

He was also masked. This mask was a face of brown bark crowned by a wreath of green holly leaves. Bright red berries were sprinkled throughout the green leaves in the crown.

Cian whispered to Anise again, "The Holly King."

The Holly King moved slowly forward, bent over, to present less of a threat. The leaves of his holly crown were fresh and green, while the leaves on the Oak King's face were starting to show signs of turning to autumn. The Oak King looked around curiously as if he wasn't aware of the presence of the other.

The Holly King rose fully upright and leapt forward to stand in front of the Oak King. Both men drew their swords. The metal of the blades glittered in the glimmering light from the lanterns. Anise gasped. The edges looked deadly sharp.

The drumbeat accelerated. Anise worried whether her

heart could keep up with the speed of the drum. The two men clashed together, and the clang of the swords filled the room.

Anise couldn't watch for a moment. Then she did look and saw that what had seemed a deadly fight could also be seen as a dance. The ringing of the blades touching each other kept time with the beat of the drum and the crowd's chanting. Each man moved back as the other moved forward, like the couples on the dance floor had done only minutes before.

The dance continued for a little until the Holly King, with a roar, the first sound either man had made, made an overhand cut through the air above the Oak King's head. There was a thud as the ends of the Oak King's antlers fell to the wooden floor.

The Oak King turned and fled out the door.

Cian whispered to Anise again, "And so, the hall of the Oak King becomes the hall of the Holly King, once more."

8

Anise felt like things were returning to normal when the summer drew to a close and the fall classes approached. Even though she'd been at the Academy for only one year, it felt like the stars were starting to align again when Vin, Jord, and Niall came back to the way-house.

Niall had reached the exalted rank of senior. This year would be his last. Vin and Jord, of course, like Anise, were returning for their second year. There were two new students at the way-house, a girl and a boy. Anise had the haughty feeling of superiority that came with having a full year of knowledge and experience under her belt.

When they checked in at registration, Anise was gratified to see that Earl had taken up her suggestion. The massive illusory head displayed in the registration hall had an eerie green cast to its complexion.

The masters took up where they had left off in the previous semester, including Master Huginn in clairvoyance. She started with a comment of appreciation for the students who had helped her collect information the last year and said she had been compiling it over the summer.

THE HALLS OF LEARNING

1

Master Huginn lifted her gaze from the paper in front of her. "As I was saying," she continued, "the information collected last year has helped us put together a picture of what happened two hundred years ago." She frowned. "Though, we still don't know why."

She brightened as she carried on. "We have learned a lot, however. This year we will be able to teach a little about the theory of clairvoyance. And, hopefully, we will also be able to begin to make a start into real-world applications."

Anise looked up at that comment. Master Huginn's unexceptionalness hadn't changed over the summer. She still made eye contact with her papers rather than with the students. Still, the prospect of learning something practical in the class caught her attention.

"So," the master continued, "there are several things for you to think about." She took a breath.

"We will be reading a book usually assigned by the channeling masters. In fact, you may be asked to read it by your channeling master. But, it turns out that it's relevant for us. How relevant we had forgotten until now.

"*The Archipelago of Dream* is assigned by channeling masters as a cautionary tale. What not to do, and why not to do it. However, with our newfound knowledge of clairvoyance, or perhaps better put, refound knowledge, we now know that clairvoyance and channeling are closely connected. The realm of dream that the channelers visit is the same realm that clairvoyants search for prophecy and truth.

"Two hundred years ago, for some reason, the masters at this academy decided to remove clairvoyance from the curriculum. They collected books from the library that referenced clairvoyance and burned them with the aid of some channeled fire imps."

"The motivation behind this extraordinary act seems to have been intentionally hidden. It seems like the masters intended for the study and practice of clairvoyance to be lost. This effort succeeded remarkably well."

Master Huginn lifted her eyes to the class. "But, now, with Master Lorenzo's encouragement, and your help, we shall make a start on restoring clairvoyance to its rightful place in the Academy."

2

Anise was lying in her bunk, reading. She had opened *The Archipelago of Dream* just before Maeve came into the dorm room. The book's first paragraph was something wholly fantastic about flying on the back of a dragon through an unfamiliar night sky over the sea of truth, looking at the shoals of dream below. Anise understood why people usually dismissed it as the writings of a crazy man.

"Anise," said Maeve, smiling, "you have a visitor."

Anise dropped the book onto her bunk and hopped to her feet. For a moment, she had the hopeful thought that someone had made the voyage across the country from Hero to see her. Then she dropped that thought as impossible and simply wondered who it could be.

This time, Maeve's smile was more private as she said, "A most handsome young man if I say so myself."

Anise gawked at her. *A handsome young man?* She wondered.

When she reached the common room, a man was there talking to Niall. Niall must have run into him while leaving to go to class. She hesitated, then ran across the room toward them.

It was Briac. He had gotten taller in the year since she had seen him last. He was dressed more respectably in refined, though still travel-worn, clothes. A lute was strapped to his back. Anise wasn't sure if it was the same lute, cleaned up, or if he had gotten a new one. There was a traveler's backpack on the ground near his feet.

His mustache had filled in. Anise thought that Uncle Sebastian wouldn't be able to say it was a little patch of dirt now. Briac's face was a little older but otherwise the same as she remembered.

She raced across the room toward him, then stopped abruptly, just a little short of where he was talking to Niall. She was overcome with shyness.

Briac stopped talking to Niall, stepped forward, and pulled her into a strong bear-hug.

"Anise!" he called out. He lifted her off the floor and spun her around in a twirl. As her feet left the ground, she wondered when he had gotten so strong.

3

Briac and Anise sat at one of the tables in the common room. They got curious looks as people came and went from the way-house, but they were reluctantly left their privacy. Briac looked more like a man and less like a boy to Anise, but she was hesitant to say so. He had no such hesitancy.

"I can't believe what a young lady you've grown into," he said admiringly. "All confident and grown-up."

"Not always so confident," said Anise, looking down at the tabletop.

"Tell me about going to school here," said Briac. He looked around the room as he spoke.

"You don't want to hear about that," said Anise, "It's just classrooms and lecturing professors. Anyway, this is just the way-house, not the Academy." She nodded at him. "I'm much more interested to hear what you've been up to. Lots of adventures, I'm sure. Where've you been? What happened to the Carnival of Wonders? Where's Elaine? Did you come all the way here just to see me?"

Briac smiled. "Well," he said, "there are some stories there. And, from all your questions, I guess you do want to hear them."

"I believe I'll answer your last question first," he said, "As the answer to that one is sort of the answer to all of them." He looked a little rueful as he continued, "I'm afraid I didn't come here just to see you. I was excited when asked to come to the Academy because I hoped I would see you here, but I'm here on an errand."

"An errand?" said Anise. "For who?"

Briac looked proud. Anise had been missing the brash boy, Briac the Magnificent. She felt like she saw him again under the thin veneer of adulthood this new Briac was wearing.

"I'm a bard!" he announced. A smile grew across his face until it stretched from ear to ear. "I sang at the Eisteddfod in Taliesin, and they picked me to join the order."

Anise was a little familiar with the order of bards. A bard was assigned to the castle of each noble or ruler in Liamec, and others wandered the roads of the land singing and telling stories. Still, she had never met anyone who had even been to their legendary city of Taliesin and had thought it just a story. The festival and musical competitions of the Eisteddfod were also fabled. The mayor of Hero had tried to call the summer market fair an Eisteddfod, but he had been laughed at.

The expression on Anise's face must have shown skepticism because the smile on Briac's broke like a wave crashing onto gray rocks on the shore.

"Well," he said quietly, "I guess I'm still just a student minstrel, but my master says I'm learning fast."

4

Maeve walked over to the table. Anise tried to hide her disappointment at the interruption. She felt like she wanted Briac all to herself, for the moment. Everyone else could talk to him later.

"Anise," said Maeve, smiling, "I hope you don't mind. I've offered that Briac can stay here for a while. Until he's done with his charge for the bardic council, at least."

Anise felt herself glowing. Then, she recognized the glow, and it turned into a flush on her cheeks.

Maeve laughed. "I guess you don't mind," she said. She turned to Briac. "And, Briac, I hope you will sing a song or two for us in the evenings. It'd be a fair way to pay for your lodgings with us."

Maeve winked at the two of them. "Well, then, I'll leave you to it." She turned and walked towards the backrooms.

There was an awkward silence. Then Briac said apologetically, "I hope I'm not intruding." He cleared his throat and continued, "The Bards and the Cunning Folk have an understanding. In fact, there's a bit of an overlap." He picked up his lute, sitting next to his backpack under the table.

"Let me show you something I'm learning how to do," he said. He started strumming the lute. The sound was soft and sweet, and she watched his fingers as he played. She wasn't sure if it was a new lute, but certainly, it had new strings and wasn't missing any, and it seemed that he had gotten better at playing since she last heard him. "Look," said Briac.

"Don't you mean, listen?" said Anise.

"I mean what I say, and I say what I mean," said Briac, while his fingers were moving smoothly on the lute strings.

Briac started singing quietly. It was a song Anise knew. The lay of the mother. It was rumored that it had been written by Liam I himself or, perhaps, by a bard at his castle. It was about his love for his mother. It always made Anise cry when she heard it. This time, though, her tears were stilled when she saw little people appearing on the tabletop. Briac's voice grew slightly strained. The tiny people, ghostly and translucent like they weren't solid, started acting out parts of the story. Anise watched in fascination as a miniature Liam cried when he said goodbye to his mother for the last time.

Briac stopped playing and rested the lute on the edge of the table. There was a bead of sweat on his forehead.

"It's still hard for me," he said. "My master says I'll get better at it."

5

Anise stared at Briac in astonishment. "It's an illusion. You're doing illusions. I felt it. I heard it in your voice. Can all bards create illusions? Is that why there's a connection between the bards and the cunning folk? What else can you do?"

Briac laughed. "Well, I'm supposed to be able to make suggestions that influence people's emotions, but I'm not very good at that one yet. It all comes out of the playing and singing."

Anise nodded. "You didn't tell me about the Carnival of Wonders and what happened with Elaine."

Briac gazed at Anise thoughtfully. "There will be time for that later," he said. "Right now, I have a favor to ask you."

Anise nodded again eagerly. "Of course," she said.

Briac hesitated like he was considering his words carefully. "Well, like I said, I am a student minstrel. There are levels and promotions within the bardic order."

Anise watched Briac's face as he spoke. His presence filled her with a feeling of calm.

"I've been given an assignment. If I complete my other training and do the assignment to my master's satisfaction, I will be promoted to the next rank." Briac pulled aside the fabric of his cloak and showed Anise a pin he wore under it. It was a tree branch cleverly crafted out of bronze. There were little bells attached to it. The bells tinkled as the fabric pulled away from the pin. They had been muffled by the cloak.

"My master asked me to travel here and do some research in the Academy library. He wants to know more about the history of a man who left the bardic order and became a master at the Academy. This was two hundred years ago. I'm not sure if they really need the information or it's just a test for me, but they want me to write a report on what happened to him here at the Academy. His books and journals are supposed to be in the library."

Anise studied Briac. "So, how can I help?" she asked.

Briac looked down at the tabletop. He flushed as he said, "I haven't told them I can't read. I've been hiding it."

Anise scrutinized Briac. She wondered how delicate she needed to be about this topic. "Is there a deadline for when you need to report back? How much time do you have to do your research?"

"Not really a deadline, no," said Briac. "I just report back when I'm done." He frowned. "Of course, I don't get promoted until I finish the report."

Anise smiled. A realization had been growing in her. This was how she could give something to Briac. "I'm going to teach you how to read!" she said excitedly. He needed more than just help on this one report; he would need this knowledge if he wanted to become a bard.

Briac's frown deepened. "I was hoping you could read the books to me," he said. "I'm not sure I can learn that."

"Of course you can," said Anise confidently. "Briac the Brilliant can learn anything!"

Soon it seemed like Briac had been in the way-house forever. Everyone liked him; everyone, except perhaps for one person. For some reason, Raphael, the cook's boy, didn't take to Briac, but no one really noticed.

Anise took Briac with her to the Academy library. Maeve had given them a pass. When they showed it to the guards at the Academy gate, they waved them on through without hesitation.

Briac stopped at the base of the stairs leading up to the library doors. "I'm not sure," he said hesitantly to Anise. "I'm not sure I should be here."

Anise snorted. "Nonsense," she said. "For one thing, Maeve said it was all right and gave you that pass. For another,

if it's all right for me to be here, it's all right for you to be."
She marched confidently up the stairs, and Briac hesitantly
followed her.

At the wide double doors, Briac paused once more
but followed Anise when she stepped assuredly through the
shimmering glow across the doorway. She hardly noticed the
glimmer anymore.

There was a thud, and Anise turned to see Briac on the
ground on the other side of the doorway, clutching his nose.

"Ow," he said.

He rose to his feet, and he and Anise inspected the
shimmering barrier across the doorway. It felt as insubstantial
as ever to Anise, but to Briac, it felt solid, though transparent.
The student working at the library front desk was watching
them with amusement. He came over and asked for Briac's
pass.

He took the pass back to the desk and did something to
the pass or the barrier. After he was done, when holding the
pass, Briac could enter and exit the doorway as easily as Anise.

They stepped together into the entrance hallway of the
library. Briac took in the marble columns, the high vaulted
ceilings, the corridors stretching off in all directions, and the
students bustling to and fro. Anise marveled again at the
majestic building. There was nothing like this in Hero.

Briac's journey to the land of the literate had begun.

6

Jord and Anise moved to the second row in Master Callum's channeling class. They weren't brave enough for the front row yet, but they wanted to be closer. When the master was done taking roll. Anise raised her hand.

The master looked up from his papers. He saw her raised hand and said, "Anise?" Anise felt like she was familiar enough with his damaged face by now to recognize a smile.

"Master Callum?" said Anise. The master made eye contact with her and nodded. Anise took a deep breath. She began, "Where do we go when we dream? What determines what spirits we meet in our dreams? Where are the spirits when we're not dreaming about them? Is the dream world we visit in our dreams the same as non-channelers visit in theirs? Why do some people channel gods and others just spirits? What's outside the circle of light?"

Master Callum's smile, insofar as it was recognizable as such, broadened. "Well, Anise," he said. "First off, did you have a nice summer?" He didn't wait for her to reply but continued, "Obviously, you spent quite a bit of it thinking about channeling."

Master Callum drew a breath himself. "Well," he said again, "I guess I'll be throwing away the lesson plan I had prepared for today."

He laughed. It was a pleasant sound. The contrast between how his laugh sounded and his face looked struck Anise again.

The master looked around at the class. "Some of the questions Anise has just asked have probably occurred to most of you," he said. "I haven't tried to answer them before now because we don't know the answers to many of them. Channeling as a discipline has evolved over time through trial and error. The trials sometimes succeed, and sometimes not, and the errors sometimes cause death or madness."

Master Callum lifted his head again and looked directly at Anise. "Gods, huh?" he said. "Ambitious, aren't we." He smiled again, "Most channeling will be affecting the spirits of people or animals. A powerful channeler will be able to speak to daemons. The most capable channelers of history were said to be able to get the attention of the gods. They don't usually listen to the likes of you or me.

"With regard to the realm of dream, most channelers believe that the place we travel to when channeling is not the same as where the non-channelers go. The dreamland that we can visit has continuity and reality. If you and I both channel the same Daemon, the description and characteristics of that Daemon will match.

"Some channelers even go as far as to speculate that the realm of dream is a real place, and it might be possible to physically travel there."

7

Briac glared at Anise indignantly. "Do you think I'm stupid?" he said. "Of course, I know that those are letters. He looked more carefully at the row of characters on the parchment in front of him. "That one's a 'z,' right?" he said.

Anise and Briac were in one of the reading alcoves in the library. Drippy was sitting in his enclosure, observing them carefully. He seemed to be hoping they wouldn't ask him to read something. A sour, moist resentment furrowed his scaly brow.

"Of course, I don't think you're stupid," said Anise. "I just need to find out what you already know so I know where to start."

"All right," said Briac. He accepted that explanation. He pointed at one of the letters on the parchment. He said eagerly, "That one's an 'x.'"

Drippy, showing a little more interest now, looked over at the parchment. The water imp shook his soggy head sadly.

Anise wasn't really sure how to go about this. She thought that maybe learning the names of the letters in the alphabet, how to recognize them, and what sounds they made would be a good beginning. She had asked if Briac would allow her to go to one of her masters for help, but he insisted that no one but her should know what they were doing in the library.

They had found a few books that might be good sources for Briac's research, but the plan for the day wasn't to do much reading. Anise wanted to start teaching Briac, and they mainly had brought the books for cover. Drippy had looked very relieved when they put the books in the reading rack but hadn't asked him to read them.

"Let's start," said Anise, "by learning to say the letters of the alphabet in order. There's a song I can teach you that helps you remember."

8

Master Videmon had them all playing with fire. Anise and Jord had taken up the same station they had last year. It felt familiar and comfortable to be back in the elemental lab. Anise felt the forces of the Key surging around inside her head as they flowed through the stone walls from the volcano. What didn't feel familiar and comfortable was the assignment that the master had given them.

"A bolt of fire or a surge of flame from a fingertip is one of the more effective tricks that an elemental mage can employ," he said. "It impresses and can be a useful weapon in times of need." He paused before continuing, "Of course, more commonly, lighting a campfire or fireplace in a house is also a useful application."

He demonstrated, producing a quick, brilliant surge of fire from his fingertips. Anise thought she could feel the heat of his flame from her station at the back of the room.

Soon there were bright flashes of light from every side. Anise noticed some particularly bright flares from the station where Vin and Orlaith were in the front. Orlaith, who Anise had thought of as the girl in purple last year, was dressed in her familiar color. She had immediately reconnected with Vin when this new year started. She hardly glanced at Anise or Jord.

Jord had no trouble with the creation of flames. She wasn't exceedingly strong in her use of fire, as she was in the control of water. Still, she could produce an adequate blaze without much difficulty.

On the other hand, Anise was struggling, as she had all of the previous year. She could feel the heat and power of the molten rock in the volcano not very far away. She could sense what the others were doing; it felt like a compelling tickle in her mind. But, all that was happening at her fingers was a little warmth.

"Close your eyes, Anise," said Jord. "Close your eyes, and let the heat flow through you. Let the fire flow from the Key, through your mind, and out your fingertips."

Anise obediently closed her eyes. She waved her fingers around a little for effect. Nothing changed.

Anise felt a weight on her shoulder. She felt something wrap around her neck. Not tightly, not threateningly, but lovingly, like a caress. She opened her eyes and scanned her own shoulder. There was nothing to be seen except for a little spiraling smoke trace. She smelled an acrid smell.

There was a touch of warmth on Anise's temple. A voice that she recognized as Iggy whispered urgently, compellingly into her ear, "Burn!"

Massive flames started shooting out of Anise's fingertips. The heat was searing, demanding, though Anise could tell that she wasn't being burned.

The flames knocked everything on the lab counter off onto the floor. The wood of the counter below the stone top started smoldering. Jord jumped back. Everyone in the lab turned to look.

Master Videmon raced over to Anise and Jord's station. He waved his hands and gestured as if pulling something down from above. A wave of water came crashing down from the ceiling dousing Jord, Anise, and everything on their workstation with an icy rain.

"There's one in every class," the master commented dryly as the water extinguished the flames.

9

Briac inspected the book in Anise's hand. "That's a kid's book." He frowned. "I may not know how to read, but I'm not a kid." Briac glanced suspiciously over at Drippy to ensure he wasn't smiling.

Anise was a little frustrated. She picked up one of the books they had brought to the reading alcove for cover. She opened it to a random page. "Well, if you're ready to read the other books, what's that word?" she asked, pointing at the page.

"Well," said Briac, "That's a 't.'" He opened his lips a little. "Tuh…"

"No," said Anise, "that's the sound that a 't' makes by itself. When it's followed by an 'h,' it sounds more like thuh." She continued, "Try reading the whole word."

Briac checked where her finger was pointing in the book. "It's too long. I can't," he said.

"It's the word thistledown," said Anise.

She picked up the beginning reader book that she had been showing Briac. "That's why we are using this book. It's not that you're a kid. It's just that it has simpler words and a less complicated structure." She smiled at Briac. "When you learned to play the lute, you didn't start with the most complicated songs? Did you?"

10

Master Devona was addressing the illusion class. Anise marveled again at how much she resembled the blonde poppet her mother had made for her when she was a child. Then she blinked. Was Master Devona letting a bit of gray show at her temples? It couldn't be her glamour slipping. She was too skilled at illusion for that. Perhaps she was trying to show her age a little to get more respect from the students.

"The trick to defeating an illusion," the master said, "is disbelief."

Cian shifted a little in her seat next to Anise.

Master Devona continued, "If you believe an illusion is real, it will influence your behavior. It can safely be ignored if you don't believe it or disbelieve it. As long as you are correct."

Anise looked around the classroom. Vin's friend Orlaith was sitting by herself at a desk in the front row. She was dressed in her usual purple. Anise wondered why Orlaith didn't like her. She didn't feel like she had done anything to make the other girl feel that way. Perhaps it was a carryover from Vin's dismissal of her sister and friends.

"The debate is strong among illusionists as to whether disbelief is a real thing or not," continued Master Devona. "Do we have a sense as to the reality of an illusion? Or, is it just a matter of convincing oneself that the thing you are perceiving isn't real."

The master frowned and looked thoughtful. "I believe, personally, that I am sensing something when I look at an illusion and believe that it is an illusion and not a real thing. Still, an argument could certainly be made that what I am sensing is simply my confidence that the perceived thing is not real.

The master laughed. The gleeful tinkling sound made Anise smile. "That said, if you disbelieve the wolf charging at you in a magical duel and ignore it to continue with your own castings, you had better be right. If it turns out that your opponent has a pet wolf or is a channeler who had a dream the night before that allowed them to control a wolf, you could be in serious trouble."

11

All the residents of the way-house were gathered in the common room. All the residents except one. Raphael was nowhere to be found. They were there to hear Briac sing a song. There was an early fall chill in the air, so a fire roared in the fireplace. The fire and lantern light in the room cast shadows over the wooden walls, the rough tables, and Briac, seated near the fire, lute on his lap.

"This one's an oldie," said the young bard. "It's called the Ill-formed Knight and the Wyvern."

His fingers moved smoothly over the strings. Gentle notes filled the air.

Leander stood before the beast,
The object of his quest.
The creature dark and serpentine,
slithered forth from its nest.

His armor shone with golden light,
His heart replete with strength,
The Ill-formed knight, the hero, born,
faced down the serpent's length.

Anise noticed tiny figures forming on the floor near the fire. She was expecting it, but she heard a gasp from one of the new students. A little knight clad in golden armor stepped forward toward the hearth. A dark scaly creature crawled from the fire, seeming to come out of it. Anise remembered the sense of intelligence she had gotten from Flambé, the dragon she had seen at the Carnival of Wonders. This creature seemed more animal-like. It felt like a snake, though it had a dragon-like head, wings, and scaled legs ending in razor claws.

The tiny knight straightened as the beast emerged from the flames. Anise felt her heart go out to the brave champion. She had always been fond of the legends of the Ill-formed Knight. Her father had told her the stories in the evenings when she was little.

A viper's hiss, a burning glare,
The wyvern seethed its wrath.
His secret doubt behind him then,
Leander saw his path.

The little golden knight braced itself on the wooden floor of the way-house.

His sword held firm, Leander's heart
was beating like a drum,
the creature leapt, its claws outstretched,
he thought his time had come.

The sword struck true, the golden suit
was drenched in serpent gore,
The cruel beast, its heart pricked through,
would plague the land no more.

Once more, the knight, Ill-formed though he was,
had managed to prevail,
The golden knight, though drenched with doubt,
was never going to fail.

12

Master Ernst wasn't any more interesting than he had been last year. But, today's alchemy class might be. They were in the lab, getting ready to work on a potion that was supposed to be able to turn someone into a frog. Jord was very excited. This was what she had been hoping to get out of Alchemy class all along.

"Why do you want to be able to turn someone into a frog?" asked Anise. She scrutinized her friend curiously. Perhaps she was about to hear something from an unexpected dark side of Jord.

"Well," said Jord, "I've always liked frogs. Maybe, if the potion is safe and temporary, I could try it on myself."

Master Ernst stressed the importance of the temporary nature of the potion. "When you make a potion," he said, "the ingredients determine the duration of the effects." He grunted a little as he looked up as if the process of raising his gray head to meet the students' eyes was an effort. "The ingredients and your inherent ability. Someone with a knack and instinct for alchemy will produce a potion with a longer-lasting and more robust effect.

"I don't want to be spending as much time as I have had to in previous classes cleaning up your mistakes."

The croaking from unhappy students and the muttered curses from the master were still ongoing when Anise got ready to leave for her next class. She left Jord at the station, cleaning mucus out of her hair. Anise thought she might not be so eager to test a potion next time.

She saw Orlaith a little ahead as she walked out the classroom door. Orlaith's purple smock was elegantly tailored and belted at the waist. Anise hurried a bit to catch up with her.

It was a rare opportunity to talk to Orlaith without Vin around. Perhaps Vin had already left.

"Orlaith," began Anise. She was a little out of breath. The taller girl turned to look at her. She looked very regal in her purple. "Why don't you like me?" Anise continued.

Orlaith's refined face looked surprised. The expression was like what you might see on a farmer if one of his pigs started speaking to him.

"Anise," she said calmly, "You're nobody. Nothing. I am Orlaith Fisher, of the North-gate Fishers."

"Fisher," said Anise excitedly, "My aunt's name was Fisher!"

"No," said Orlaith dismissively, and she turned and walked out of the lab.

13

Briac put the book down with a sigh. Anise smiled at him and said, "That's amazing! You just finished that whole book!" Even Drippy looked proud. He flapped his scaly wings in his enclosure. Anise reached up to wipe a drop of Drippy slime off her cheek.

"It's just a kid's book," said Briac.

"Well," said Anise, "every journey begins with a first step, and every book reading begins with the first page."

The rest of the school year flew by for Anise. She enjoyed her lessons with Briac but realized that she was teaching him the skill he would need to leave. Once he could puzzle through the books he needed to finish his assignment, he would head back to his bardic master to continue his training.

As finals started creeping up on her, she was torn. Sebastian had promised that he would make the journey to escort her back to Hero for the summer this year. Even if it wasn't practical, she would be able to spend some amount of time at home. Anise was excited to see her Aunts, Rose and Isabel.

On the other hand, that would mean leaving while Briac was still laboring his way through his task. She wanted to be able to help him complete the job.

Briac was working on reading the journals and other books that referenced his subject. Anise was still standing by, ready to help when needed. Still, he was getting better and better at pushing through the material. The key, he had learned, was to be patient when he was having difficulty with a word and stop and work on it until he was ready to go on.

A picture was forming of who the man Briac was studying had been. His name was Drun Coeloc, and as Briac had told Anise, he had left the bardic order to become a master at the Academy. Interestingly enough, he was listed on the Academy rolls as a master of Musicology. A subject of which he was the first and only master that Anise and Briac could find in the Academy's history.

The source material in the library that referenced him was intermittent and spotty. His personal journals were there, though some pages had been removed.

His journals referenced his reasons for coming to the Academy. However, the missing pages were frequent throughout this section of the book. He felt that there was some clear danger to the land of Liamec, or perhaps to the whole world, though he used the word creation. From reading what was left of the journals, one got the impression that he felt he was the only one who could save the world from this danger. He thought his coming to the Academy would be part of that help.

That was when the letter from Uncle Sebastian came.

UNDER THE EARTH

1

T he first thing that Anise understood from the letter was that her uncle wasn't coming to take her home. Her initial reaction was a feeling of disappointment. *How could he? He'd promised.* Then she read further and understood why he wasn't coming.

Twilight was missing. Aunt Isabel and Uncle Sebastian had taken him on a luncheon in a field by a forest. It wasn't clear from the letter if they had fallen asleep or if he had just snuck off while they were momentarily unaware. But, either way, the baby had wandered off into the woods.

This happened a week ago. The rest of the searchers had given up, but Sebastian wasn't going to. He sounded like he would be out there every day throughout the summer, searching.

Uncle Sebastian asked Anise to understand why he wouldn't be able to meet her. He hoped there might be something the masters at the Academy could do, some magic they might be able to apply, to help find their baby.

Anise was in tears before she finished the letter. She thought about her willful, difficult charge and couldn't imagine how lonely and terrified he must feel.

After her alchemy final, Anise approached Master Ernst. "I'm sorry for your loss," he said gruffly in his scratchy voice. "I'm afraid I'm not much of a hand at finding."

"Finding?" asked Anise.

"It falls under clairvoyance," said the master, "I took a class in it long ago. I never got the hang of it."

Master Videmon wasn't much help either. "Elemental

magic is pretty much here and now," he said. "You need something a little more mystical. It sounds more like clairvoyance to me, as well." He frowned sympathetically, "It's too bad it happened now. We might have relearned how to do it in a few years."

Master Huginn agreed. "The science of clairvoyance and the specific application of finding would be the right thing to apply to this question. Unfortunately, as you know, they're lost." She met Anise's eyes sorrowfully, "I'm afraid I have no idea how to help you."

2

Anise woke from a deep sleep in her dorm room. She had the sad thought that this room was starting to feel more familiar than her bedroom in Aunt Rose's house in Hero. Then she noticed that the other bunks were missing and that she was in the circle of light of a channeling dream.

She sat up and looked around the room. The walls blocked the edges of the circle, and the light flickered like candlelight. Now though, she knew that if the walls hadn't been there, there would still have been a barrier of darkness at her dream's boundary.

Anise felt the distant presence of the Watcher, but something was blocking his attention. She knew that he couldn't tell what was happening in her dream.

Helios stood in the center of the room. His crown, and his youthful, proud face beneath it, shone with a warm, bright light.

"Anise," he said. "You're sad. How can I help?"

"Lord Helios," said Anise. She paused, trying not to cry. The sympathy he was showing her made it harder, not easier.

"It's my ..." She hesitated, "... brother, Twilight."

Lord Helios stood calmly, gazing at her, waiting for her to continue.

"He's missing."

Helios blinked. Part of the light shining from him that flooded the room was coming from his eyes. When he blinked, the lighting in the room changed a little.

"Seeing as you see everything under the sun," Anise continued. "I was hoping you could look for him."

"Of course," said the god quietly. He closed his eyes again. His handsome shut-eyed face looked still, then thoughtful, then he reopened his eyes.

"I'm sorry, Anise," he said, "I wish I had better news for you." He frowned. "As you said, as you know, I see everything under the sun, everything under the light of day."

The god stepped forward and put his hand on Anise's shoulder. The featherweight touch felt warm, like the light of a spring day.

"He hasn't been under the light of day since he was lost. He hasn't been under the sun since then. Since he isn't under the sun, he must be under the earth."

3

Since hearing the sad news that Twilight was gone, Anise had had difficulty feeling anything. Seeing as Sebastian wasn't coming to take her home, she could help Briac complete his project. She felt like she should be happy about this. The emotion wouldn't come.

Niall was leaving after completing his final year at the Academy. Anise had never formed the connection with him that she had wanted. It didn't matter. She felt like the presence of his handsome face had been like a painting on the wall. Something she had been able to admire from a distance.

Jord tried to cheer her up before she and her sister left for the summer. Anise appreciated the effort, but the reality left her cold.

Anise couldn't bring herself to write Uncle Sebastian what Helios had said. She just wrote to him that the magic of the Academy had been unable to locate Twilight.

It wasn't until the Midsummer festival, the Litha, came again to the way-house that Anise started to recover. She hid at the library with Briac as Maeve and Cian's relatives again prepared the event. When they came back to the way-house, Maeve served them chouchen.

They danced with the revelers, watched the battle between the Holly King and the Oak King, and had perhaps one drink more than they should have.

Later, when Briac was escorting Anise back to her dorm room down the wooden corridor, he turned and kissed her gently on the lips.

Raphael's head of tousled red hair disappeared back into the doorway just as Briac turned toward it.

"Goodnight, Anise," said Briac quietly as he crossed the

hall to the boy's dorm.

As the students were all off for the summer, Anise and Briac had the library almost to themselves. They spent more time than perhaps they should have in their favorite reading alcove with Drippy the water imp.

Anise felt Drippy had started to recognize them, though he never said a word unless they asked him to read. When they came into his alcove, his moist leathery wings would flap in what she thought of as a friendly manner.

Anise didn't mention anything about the summer solstice kiss to Briac, though she did spend quite a bit of time thinking about it. However, in a momentary break from poring over the journals of Drun Coeloc, she did ask him about his time with the Carnival of Wonders and how it had ended.

"Oh," said Briac, "that's not much of a story. Did I ever tell you what happened with Flambé, the Carnival's dragon?"

"No," said Anise hesitantly.

"She kept getting bigger," said Briac cheerfully. "Eventually, the folk of the Carnival weren't sure what to do with her." He looked thoughtful. "She might have really been a dragon. In the end, she was growing lumps between her shoulder blades that could have been the starts of wings."

"What did they do?"

"She took it out of their hands. One morning Elaine came out to Flambé's cage, and she was gone. She'd broken the bars like they were twigs. She must have been growing stronger even faster than she was growing bigger."

"But you and Elaine?" insisted Anise.

"Like I said, not very interesting. I think Elaine just got tired of me. We were in Taliesin for the Eisteddfod, so it worked out well for me."

Anise regarded Briac a little skeptically. She was sure there was more to the story that he wasn't telling her. She thought about pressing the issue, but it was clear that he didn't want to talk about it. Reluctantly, she dropped the question.

4

Briac finished his report on the mysterious Drun Coeloc. There were gaps in their understanding of what had happened and his motives, but the basics were there. Anise helped him write the final version. His reading had gotten passable, and he was working on writing, but his handwriting was not yet a thing of beauty.

Two hundred years ago, Drun had thought that something catastrophic was happening at the Academy. And that he was the only one who could solve the problem. He had acquired this idea while engaged as a bard in Taliesin. Briac was initially confused about this. "There's not really a connection between things at Taliesin and the Academy. At least there isn't now," he said.

Drun had, apparently with the bardic council's blessing, traveled to the Academy and petitioned for a master's position. Somehow he had been successful at this. He had been the only professor of musicology the Academy had ever had.

There were missing pages and inked-out paragraphs in the records from before Drun became a master, but they increased after. It was hard to form a picture of his career after he had become a master. There was an impression that he had been respected and listened to but no clear indication of why.

One thing that Anise found strange was frequent references to something called dragonfell. It seemed Drun had some process for turning this material into cloth and made his clothes out of it. It seemed odd how much this was emphasized in his journals, so Anise did some research. In an old herbology reference work, she found that dragonfell was a word for thistledown.

The timing of when Drun came to the Academy struck Anise as curious. He had arrived at the Academy not long before the time Master Huginn had been researching for Clairvoyance class. Anise kept an early draft of Briac's report to show to her when the school year started.

Once Briac finished his report, nothing was keeping him in Ashton. When they said goodbye, Anise and Briac pretended that they would see each other soon. They seemed to be pretending further, or perhaps it was part of the same pretense, that parting wasn't a serious thing.

However, as Briac stepped out the door of the way-house, he kissed Anise lightly on the lips. His lips felt warm. Then he turned and headed down the street, his lute and his travel backpack on his back.

Anise stood in the doorway, watching him walk away. Maeve stepped up behind her and put her hand on Anise's back. When Briac went out of view, Anise turned to Maeve, buried her head in the older woman's shoulder from above, and started crying.

5

Anise and Jord were third-years. They knew the superiority of the upperclassman. They looked around the green the first day they walked to classes and marveled at how young the first-years looked. Jord felt wise. Anise felt old.

"They look like little kids," said Jord. "Look, they don't even know where their classes are."

"We don't know where all of ours are either," said Anise. Her class list looked the same as last year, except for an optional class that she had added at Maeve's suggestion. It was a training class for students to learn to be able to physically defend themselves. Jord had signed up with her.

"You mean the fighting class?" said Jord. "I don't know why Maeve made us take that. We're going to be mages, not brawlers. We don't need that stuff."

"It might be useful," said Anise.

At dinner that evening, Anise looked around at her fellow way-house residents. She, Cian, Vin, and Jord, were now the elders. Except for Maeve, of course. The new students were chattering excitedly among themselves. Anise sighed to herself; she felt the weight of her years.

Raphael stepped up next to her and put a plate down in front of her. Her eyes caught on his arm in its white cotton cook's tunic. Had he been putting on a little muscle?

She looked back at him and met his eye. He'd been getting taller as well. He'd been in the way-house with her all summer, but she hadn't noticed. His unruly mop of red hair was a little long. As he straightened up from putting the plate down, she resisted the urge to reach out and either muss it up further or smooth it flatter.

"How are you doing, Raffy?" she asked.

Raphael glanced sideways at her, smiled shyly, and nodded his head. Then he moved on to put a plate in front of Jord.

6

Anise stood at the end of a line of girls. Some were giggling, though Anise didn't see how they could be. She was dressed in a cotton blouse and a skirt that was the lightest she had in her small collection of clothes. Jord was down at the other end of the line. As they had come into the room, talking, the woman now standing in front of them had separated them. She made Jord move across the room to the other side. She had done the same with other girls who had come in together.

It was a woman, though Anise hadn't been sure at first. She was wearing strange clothes. Red from head to toe. She wore a red cloth top, loosely belted at the waist by a strip of fabric, and red cotton leggings. Anise had rarely seen a woman out in public in leggings. Though, when she had visited the Carnival of Wonders, some people were dressed very unusually.

But it wasn't just the clothes that had made Anise unsure if she was a woman. Her head was shaved, and Anise had also rarely seen a woman without long hair. At first, she had confused Anise, but her face was beautiful and a little exotic. Her features were delicate, and she had charming brown eyes and long lashes. The shaved head made the delicacy of her features stand out.

She was a little loud, however. Barking out orders, she strode down the line of girls, poking at dresses, commenting on shoes, and, in general, making people uncomfortable.

The room was high-ceilinged, and the floor was smooth and polished. It didn't look polished with age; it had been buffed and waxed until it shone.

The woman stopped examining people and stepped to the front, turning to face the line of girls.

"I am not a master at this Academy," she announced. Proudly, it seemed. "I am your trainer, instructor in the physical arts, worst enemy, and best friend." She looked over the line of girls. "You will call me teacher or Sifu."

The teacher pointed to a pile of folded red clothes. "Next time, we will dress more appropriately. For now, however, I will make you sweat in what you are wearing."

7

Master Huginn was as interested as Anise had thought she would be in Briac's report. "We didn't find this information because it doesn't mention clairvoyance," she said. "But what if all those references were in the missing pages and inked-out areas? The timing's very interesting."

"I have a theory," said Anise.

The master glanced up from the report and looked expectantly at her.

"I think Master Coeloc was the one who started the Academy down the path of eliminating clairvoyance. He brought them some news or information that made them feel like they needed to do it. The timing's just right. There was enough time between when he arrived and when they burned the books for them to have confirmed something he told them."

Anise started to feel powerful. She had confidence that she could decide whether or not she would have a channeling dream. Although she got into the habit of suppressing channeling dreams to avoid the gaze of the Watcher. She had the knowledge to produce illusions that could deceive and confuse, though she had worries about whether or not this was a form of lying.

In alchemy class, the potions they were producing were more effective and powerful than ever before. Though, they were also harder to concoct. Master Ernst encouraged them to use their elemental skills to help brew potions. Fire to heat. Air and wind to desiccate, and so forth. "It's the only thing elemental magic is good for," he said.

Anise wasn't so sure. Her burgeoning elemental skills

were a big part of what made her feel powerful. Now that Iggy had helped her free herself from her fire blockage, the ability to shoot forth a bolt of flame from her fingertip was exciting. Not to mention controlling the flow of water, earth, or wind. Being able to manipulate the elements made her feel like she could influence the world around her.

That's when the next letter from home arrived.

UNDER THE SUN

1

The letter was written by Uncle Sebastian. He told Anise that he had some good news to share. Her Aunt Isabel had given birth to a baby girl. Her name was Sunshine, but they were calling her Sunny for short.

Uncle Sebastian went on to say that Sunshine would never replace Twilight. Not in the world or in their hearts. Still, he was pleased to see a smile on Isabel's face again.

Anise did a quick calculation and figured out that Isabel must have been pregnant on the outing where Twilight was lost.

With the letter came a small wooden box. It was beautifully inlaid with different woods, and Anise was sure that Isabel's mother, Mrs. Fisher, had made it. She took a moment to open it and remove a small sealed vial before reading on.

"The vial in the box we sent you along with this letter is a gift from Lilith. She suggests you drink it after you finish reading."

Anise inspected the vial and held it up to the afternoon sunlight streaming through the window. The liquid inside was clear and looked slightly thicker than water when she tilted the vial.

Sebastian went on to provide some more news. Aunt Rose, he wrote, had been courting or perhaps was being courted. Anise stopped reading again. She took a moment to wrap her head around this concept.

"Mr. Shepherd, the miller, and Rose have been seen about town together," the letter continued. "At first, I was surprised, but Rose says he has an inner sweetness that he hides behind a gruff exterior."

The letter ended with expressions of how much

everyone was missing her. Isabel and Rose sent their love. Anise put down the paper.

She picked up the vial and pulled out the cork; it came off with a light "pop." The liquid inside smelled like nutmeg. She drank it down.

Anise's vision grew cloudy. She blinked her eyes, trying to see. Then she could again. What she saw was the smiling image of a young baby. The baby's face was close: as if she was holding it in her arms. Bright blue eyes, traces of thin blond hair, and a clear light complexion surrounded that sunny smile. She heard a cooing sound, the baby reached up a tiny hand, and Anise felt a warm grip on her thumb. She gazed into those bright blue eyes for a moment. Then she blinked again, her vision cleared, and the baby was gone.

2

Anise awoke in a sun-dappled meadow in a clearing in the woods. The clearing reminded her of places she had explored in the forests outside the little town of Hero. In fact, she supposed, in some ways, it *was* a clearing in the woods outside of her hometown.

She rose from the soft bed of grass she had been lying on and looked around, satisfied at her success. Master Callum had instructed the channeling class with more details about how the circle of light worked.

"I have already warned you never to leave your circle," he had said, "but that doesn't mean you can't have some control over it. The instinct to not even approach the edge is strong in every channeler I have ever worked with, but it is, after all, still a dream. By default, your circle of light, your safe haven in the dreaming realm, resembles where you went to sleep, but it doesn't have to. You can control how your circle appears. It's related to dream-walking. When I want to dream-walk, I manipulate my circle of light to be yours, which brings me to you."

Anise looked across the sun and shadow dappled grass at an approaching figure. It was Helios. For the first time, the brightness of his crown didn't outshine everything. The light streaming down from above the trees lining the edges of her circle was as bright.

As usual, the presence of Helios made her feel safe from the attention of the Watcher.

"Anise," said Helios, "what do you need?"

"Lord Helios," said Anise, "I have a new ..." She hesitated. "... sister."

"I know," said the sun god with a smile. His smile brightened the sunlight in the clearing. "Her name pleases me."

"I want to give her something. I want to protect her, to love her. I was hoping you could help me with a gift for her worthy of her name." Anise glanced down at the grass. "I know that I have a limit on the number of times I can beg your favor, but this is important to me."

"Anise," said the sun god, "you have just begun your account with me." He gazed at her and continued. "Look to the sun for a gift for your sister."

3

Anise was leaving the way-house the following morning when something made her stop. She was supposed to be meeting Jord at Alchemy class, and she was running a little late. Still, something about how the morning sunlight shone through the front windows drew her attention.

The sunlight streaming through the windows at an angle onto the wooden floor looked solid. It seemed almost like it might be firm enough to touch.

Anise stepped over nearer the window. Dust motes floated in the golden light that pressed its way across the floor. She looked down at the floorboards. One knot in one of the boards shone with reflected light like it was made of something other than wood.

Anise reached down and felt the surface of the knot. It was raised a little above the rest of the floorboard wood. She touched the edge, lifted, and picked up a circular object that shone as she raised it.

It was a golden medallion. Shaped like a coin, one side had a wood grain pattern, as if from the knot in the floorboard, and the other showed the face of Helios in profile. A smooth link-less golden chain was attached to one edge.

It was beautiful. Small enough that it might be worn by a young child, the patterned surface glinted in the light. As Anise moved her hands, the golden chain flowed like water through her fingers.

Anise felt the attention of the sun god and knew what the medallion would do and how it would help the wearer.

The medallion would draw just enough of the sun god's attention to the wearer that his sight of everything that happened under the sun would warn them of danger. Any threat that was under the light of day would sound an alarm.

Anise felt that it was a very fitting gift for her new relative.

4

A nise looked down the line of red-clad girls. *Not girls,* she thought. *We're all away from home studying to be mages. I should be thinking of us as women.* She felt a surge of pride gazing at the group of women.

"Sifu," said Anise, raising her hand carefully. "When are you going to teach us how to use weapons?"

The teacher turned to Anise, her delicate features flashing briefly through a smile before firming up into a look that was supposed to be stern. She stood in front of the line of women.

"In this world, and especially as women in this world, we are not always armed. You will, on occasion, have to face someone with bad intent who has a weapon when you don't."

She softened her tone. "That said, I will be teaching you the use of some common weapons once I feel like you all have a basic idea of how to respond to an attack. This class aims to teach you to be able to defend yourselves against attack, not to attack others."

Jord was lined up next to Anise. Their teacher had softened her stance on girls who knew each other standing near one another once they had learned to respect her rules.

The two of them paired up as often as they could on the bout mat, though that was a little frowned upon.

"You need to learn to face different opponents. It will most likely be against someone unfamiliar that you find these skills called upon in the real world. It's best to have a different opponent for each match."

For the first several classes, Sifu had been asked why they should learn to fight physically when they could just use magic to defend themselves.

"As you have all learned from your classes, your

masters, and your own experiences, casting illusions and focusing elemental forces drain stamina. There may come a time when you have no more energy for magic, and yet you are still in a position where you need to defend yourself." She blinked her long lashes. "Also, those who are stronger as alchemists and channelers have skills that don't lend themselves directly to fights."

5

That spring, Anise's feeling of increasing power grew. But, along with it came the idea that the abilities she was acquiring could be used for everyday things as well. When she was asked to light the fireplace in the common room on a chilly evening, she didn't think to try and reach for the tinderbox. Instead, she made contact with the element of fire. A blazing flame shooting from the tip of her finger made the old box feel obsolete.

When Cookie complained about an invasion of mice in the kitchen, Anise dreamt her way into their furry little minds and cleared the problem that way. She convinced the little mouse clan's leader that life would be better somewhere else, and the rest followed.

Anise's feeling of power and control grew in all of her classes but one. In Master Huginn's clairvoyance class, the master and students started approaching an understanding of clairvoyance techniques. However, none of them became very proficient at the practice.

The clairvoyants of old had methods of trancing themselves into states where their perception left their bodies. Meditation and the judicious use of certain herbs allowed them to sit in a room, take a spiritual journey to another plane, and return with insights and visions.

Anise couldn't help but detect a similarity to the journey into the world of dreams that channelers took. One difference, however, was that the clairvoyants described their trips as journeys along paths. They talked about these routes as clear, well-marked, and well-trodden. Like channelers with their circle of light, the clairvoyants warned against leaving the marked paths until you reached the end.

The path of life, the path of family, and of death. There were many paths, each with its own method of trancing, its own herbs, and incense. And, importantly, its own truths to be learned.

But as spring started to turn into summer, Anise's thoughts weren't on either her growing powers or the upcoming exams. Sebastian had promised to come to get her and escort her home for the break. She would get to see Aunt Rose, Aunt Isabel, her friend Mary, and she would get to meet Sunshine for real.

6

Anise packed. She didn't own much and couldn't carry much with her anyway. But there were things she wanted to take and things she felt she had to. Helios's amulet: her gift for Sunshine, was placed in a position of honor and safety at the bottom of her pack.

She had little gifts as well for Rose and Isabel. She didn't have any money. It had been a source of embarrassment when Vin and her friend Orlaith went on their frequent shopping expeditions to Ashton's market. She had never felt comfortable joining them. Though they knew that she didn't have any money, showing it by being on a shopping trip without buying anything was more than she was comfortable with. Jord went with them sometimes.

She had done odd jobs for Maeve, sometimes for small change. That's how she had saved up enough to buy her presents.

It didn't matter. Uncle Sebastian was coming; she was going home. Her heart started beating faster when she thought about seeing Aunt Rose again for the first time in almost three years.

Anise thought that she would miss Maeve and Cian this summer, and maybe Cookie and Rafael, but that thought paled next to the excitement she felt.

Finals and the departures of the other students blew past. Everything faded into a blur that ended the afternoon when Maeve called her to the front door. A dusty Sebastian stood there, holding the lead of an even dustier Betsy.

Anise had prepared by loading a couple of carrots into her belt. Still, when the reality of standing in front of her uncle hit, she was suddenly shy. He looked older. He looked older, a little tired, and a little sad. Though, his face lit up when he saw her.

Betsy called out, "Heee Awwww," her familiar mule bray, and started pushing at Anise's smock near the carrots in her belt. Sebastian dropped the lead, stepped forward, and enfolded Anise in his strong arms.

7

The journey to Hero flew by. Anise remembered the trip out to Ashton three years ago as an odyssey. A hazardous, dangerous trek. It was almost disappointing how smoothly the return trip went. It took time, of course. She had plenty of time to reconnect with her uncle and her favorite mule.

Sebastian was very interested in what she had learned at the Academy. She described channeling class, alchemy, what they had learned about clairvoyance, and showed him a few simple illusions. Sebastian was most impressed, however, with her elemental mastery of fire. He assigned her the task of lighting the campfires in the evenings. Every time he watched a little burst of flame shoot out of her fingertip, he would say, "Now, *that's* useful."

Betsy was initially pleased to see Anise as well. Though, once she ran out of fresh carrots, their relationship returned to pretty much what it was before. Anise sized up both Sebastian and Betsy and felt that it might have been the man that had aged more in the last years.

One evening as they sat around the campfire, Sebastian asked Anise a question that it seemed had been on his mind.

"Why'd I have to come to get you, Anise?" he asked.

Anise felt sad. "Because I wanted to come home, and I thought you wanted me home," she said.

"No," said Sebastian, with a shake of his head, "that's not what I meant. Of course, we want you home." He put his hand on top of hers. "No, what I meant was, why didn't you fly home, ride home on a dragon, or vanish in one place and reappear in another?"

Anise was relieved at his explanation. "Well," she said, "no one knows how to fly, though there are air elementalists who have been working on it." She shook her own head. "I'm not sure what discipline would lead to the disappearing thing, and no one's seen a dragon for two hundred years."

Anise stopped short. Suddenly a thought occurred to her. Her own words echoed in her mind. *Two hundred years. That couldn't be a coincidence.*

Sebastian didn't notice her momentary distraction. "Well," he said, "we'll just have to learn how to ride horses."

8

After they set up their camp the night before they were due to arrive in Hero, Sebastian pulled a little vial out of his pocket. There were two liquids in the vial, one colored blue and one colored yellow, separated by a thin barrier. The vial was cleverly constructed. There was a catch on the side that, if loosened, would allow the fluids to mix.

"What's that?" asked Anise.

"It's a potion that Lilith gave me," said Sebastian. "Although, she said it wasn't really a potion cause a potion is usually something you drink." He released the catch on the side and shook the little vial. The yellow and blue fluids mixed together, making a clear fluid with an emerald green color. Betsy observed the transformation carefully, wondering if the green liquid might not be a new kind of grass.

"She said that if I do this, a little bottle of similar stuff on one of her shelves will turn the same color," said Sebastian. "She will be watching it and should know that we're almost home. That way, they can meet us." He shook his head. "I made the mistake of asking her how it worked. When she said something about spooky action at a distance, I stopped listening."

Anise thought that she'd be able to talk about some trade secrets with Lilith. It seemed that maybe the cunning folk did have some knowledge that the mages of the academy didn't share.

People were waiting to meet them when they got to the town gates. Anise felt like the whole town was there. She looked around to see who had come. Her vision was obscured by a vast sweep of pink linen.

"Anise," cried Aunt Rose as she hugged her niece so

tightly that Anise had trouble breathing. "You're home." When her breathing resumed, Anise found herself held out at arm's length by her aunt. With a shock, she noticed that they were the same height.

"Let me look at you," said Rose. Teardrops were hiding in the corners of her eyes, and her voice was a little shaky. "My, how you've grown." Anise took in her aunt as her aunt scrutinized her. She wondered how someone could change so much in such a short time and yet still be exactly the same.

A man stood behind Rose, seeming to Anise like he wanted to have his hand on her aunt's shoulder. It was the miller, Mr. Shepherd. Anise wondered why he looked different to her. Then she realized that he was smiling.

The rest of Anise's welcome went by in a blur. Of course, they hadn't been able to get through the event without a speech from the mayor. He had had banners made up. He must have asked someone how to spell her name because they read simply and surprisingly tastefully, "Welcome home, Anise!"

"Our brave town of Hero," said the mayor, "having already acquired a champion for the ages." He swept his hand in front of Sebastian. "Now boasts an Academy-trained mage among its ranks as well."

Even more than when she left to go to the Academy, Anise wondered who he thought he was talking to. Half the town was there, but half the town was still less than half the crowd at one of the Carnival of Wonder's performances.

Of course, Isabel, Lilith, Mary, and Isabel's mother, Mrs. Fisher, were there. Still, Anise felt a unique rush of excitement when she met Sunshine for the first time. Isabel was holding her in her arms. The little baby tugged at Anise's attention with her wispy blond hair and bright blue eyes.

"Wait a minute, Aunt Isabel," said Anise. She opened her backpack and pulled out the amulet. It had been moved to the top to be easy to find. The metal glinted in the sunlight as she put the chain carefully over the baby's neck. Sunny cooed and reached out a hand toward the shiny thing as it was lowered toward her. "May it always keep you safe," Anise whispered.

Aunt Rose called for Anise's attention once more. She stood beside Mr. Shepherd, with his hand on her shoulder this time.

"Anise," she said, "we have something to tell you."

9

Sebastian told Anise a little about how Rose and Mr. Shepherd had gotten together. It had started with a feud over who would be making the baked goods for the little town of Hero. Mr. Shepherd had been baking bread with the flour from his mill until Rose came to town. It started with the feud and ended with Rose's rhubarb pie. Once Rose got Mr. Shepherd hooked on her rhubarb pie, the battle was as good as won.

The wedding was a bright, sunny, happy affair. Mr. Shepherd and his daughter Mary had become Rose's assistants at the bakery instead of the competition, so the cakes, pastries, and other foodstuffs were plentiful and delicious.

Anise got to escort her aunt down the aisle. It was a little unconventional, but both Anise and Rose wanted it that way. So, Mr. Shepherd, or Byram as he now insisted Anise call him, didn't dream of fighting it.

As soon as she noticed that she was missing, Anise asked Mr. Shepherd (Byram) about his older daughter, Anne. The smile that was a permanent part of his face nowadays wavered. He mumbled that he didn't want to talk about it.

Mary tried to fill Anise in. "Anne ran off with an outlaw," she said excitedly. Mr. Shepherd's smile, which had been starting to come back, wavered. He scowled at Mary. She glanced down at the ground. "Papa doesn't like to talk about it. I worry about her."

Aunt Rose moved into the mill house, Byram Shepherd's home. It was a large stone house attached to the mill. It was one of the grandest homes in Hero, but since Mr. Shepherd's first wife, Anne and Mary's mother, died, it had become a little neglected.

They found a little room for Anise to stay in while she was there for the break. Anise found it strange at first. The room shuddered and shook with the grinding of the mill and the turning of the wheel. She could also hear the water running outside her window. It became a lullaby after a few days, and she slept better than she had in years.

There was a small mossy spot between the bottom of the mill wheel and the mill's stone wall, just above the smaller pond where the water flowing over the wheel started its journey toward the river. It wasn't visible from the lane that crossed the stream a little below. You had to clamber down a slope and duck under the moving axle of the mill wheel to get there. Still, it was dry unless the stream was flowing more than usual. And the luxurious green moss made a soft cushion on which to sit if you were so inclined.

It was Mary's particular spot to hide from her father and spend time alone. Of course, now that her best friend was also her sister, she sat there with Anise with the afternoon sun shining down on them.

"Tell me about Anne," said Anise. "Did she really run off with an outlaw?"

Mary shook her head. "I want to hear about the Academy," she said. "Show me some magic."

Anise reached over towards Mary's ear and pantomimed pulling something out of it. A large gold coin dropped through the air and fell to the mossy ground. It looked like it indented the moss.

Mary gasped. "Is it real?" she said as she reached out toward the coin.

"Of course not," said Anise. She waved her hand, and the coin disappeared.

Mary looked disappointed. "Why not?" she said.

"Well," said Anise, "it has to do with the littlest bits of

stuff. You can move them around and change them a bit, but making new ones out of nothing isn't something we can do."

She smiled at her new sister. "I'll tell you more later if you want to know. I really need to hear about Anne."

10

Sebastian and Anise spent part of that summer learning how to ride. Sebastian didn't own any horses, but the mayor generously offered to share some town resources to help out. He asked Mr. Thatcher, the farrier, to provide Anise and Sebastian with the loan of a pair of horses for learning and the trip back to school.

Betsy was not happy with the newcomers in Sebastian's barn. She reluctantly put up with the cows, but these newcomers, snorting and neighing, were more than she could bear. She went on a food strike initially, but then she got hungry, and that ended.

Anise adored riding. She felt a bond with her horse and loved spending time with her uncle. She named her horse Quickly because she enjoyed saying things like, "Let's go, Quickly," or, "I'm going to ride Quickly."

Anise and Sebastian learned to ride. Anise learned to ride Quickly. By the time the break was rolling to an end, they were riding well enough that they would be able to make the trip on horseback.

Betsy wasn't going to be able to come. She wouldn't be able to keep up with the horses. Anise dreaded the day that she had to say goodbye.

Saying goodbye to everyone was hard. Sunny grabbed Anise's finger, as she had in the vision from Lilith's potion, and wouldn't let go. Rose cried again. Anise cried too.

The trip back to school went even quicker than the trip to Hero. Soon enough, Anise was back at the way-house saying goodbye to her uncle. Quickly turned around to look at her inquiringly as Sebastian rode off, holding on to his lead.

If Anise hadn't known better, she might have thought that he had tears in his eyes, like she did in hers.

DRAGON'S GULLET AUDITORIUM

1

Anise and Jord discussed their final projects. As part of your last year at the Academy, you submitted a final project in your chosen field of study. Jord and Vin were working together with Master Videmon. Anise was planning her project with Master Callum.

Jord and Vin kept their project secret. This was the first time she told Anise anything about it. "You have to promise not to tell anyone, Anise," she said. "Vin and Master Videmon want it to be a secret until we demonstrate it to the other masters."

Master Videmon's theories about twins had a lot to do with how they interacted with magic. He had been fascinated with Jord's abilities with water and Vin's with fire. His belief in the connection between the twins and his knowledge of elemental magic had led to Vin and Jord's final project.

"We've invented a new element," said Jord. "We call it firter." She looked shyly at the floor. "You know, for fire and water put together. I came up with that." She got excited. She hadn't liked keeping her work from Anise, and she was eager to share her knowledge.

"It turns out that water is made up of parts. Too small to see. But, when you take the tiny parts of water apart, both sides of it want to burn." She lifted her hand and drew a little spiraling line in the air. A string of water rippled in the air behind her finger. Then she concentrated, holding her other hand out and spreading the fingers around the floating stream of water. The water sprang into flame but kept flowing.

It was like a gleaming, burning snake writhing above Jord's hand in the air. They were far enough away from the Key to the elements that Jord was drawing the moisture and heat from the air. Anise could feel the air drying out. She shivered.

"You take the parts of each little bit of water apart, burn its parts, then put it back together again," said Jord. "It took both Vin and me to figure out how to do it, but I can do it a bit by myself now." Jord stopped concentrating and dropped her hands to her sides. The fiery writhing snake fizzled a bit as it disappeared.

"Master Videmon is trying to figure out if there's a use for it. Still, he was very excited that we figured out how to do it," said Jord.

2

Channeling class had become a bit boring. Master Callum spent most of his time warning the class about things they shouldn't do and things they should be wary of. "The spirits and souls you encounter in the dreaming are not your friends and will not always be under your control," he said.

"For example," Master Callum's face took on a severe look, though, as always, it was a little hard to distinguish expressions on his damaged face. "The spirits of the dead and the daemons of death are dark and dangerous. Even if you are powerful enough to channel them, you probably shouldn't. Interaction with the daemons of death can leave a shadow on your soul."

Master Callum's voice took on a somber tone. "I had personal experience with this when I was a student like you. I had a friend. A young man; friendly, charming. Generally a happy sort. He specialized in channeling the darker spirits. Over the time I knew him, he changed from a cheerful young man into a bitter unfriendly soul. I'm not sure if it was entirely the channeling of death spirits that led him down this path, but it certainly felt like it."

Master Callum proceeded, "There are some that can do it. Our own Master Lorenzo, the head of the channeling department, has power over the darker spirits. As we all know and trust, his soul is still free of darkness and taint."

"Anyway," the master concluded, "Though it has its uses, the channeling of the daemons of death is probably best left to those with the propensity for it."

Later, Anise spoke to Master Callum about her idea for a final project.

"That's very ambitious, Anise," he said. "As we've discussed in class, conjuring an artifact from a channeling dream is quite possible."

He continued, "It's said that the spirits don't like leaving items behind when their channeling missions are done. They think of it as messy. As unfinished business." Master Callum frowned, "Though, even that may be dependent on the power and presence of the channeler."

Anise had been inspired by her gift for Sunshine. When thinking about what to do for her own final project, the shiny golden amulet she had given her sister kept coming to mind.

Somehow, though, she couldn't bring herself to talk to Master Callum about Helios. She spoke of a sun daemon. She knew that the power of the spirit you conjured in your channeling dreams reflected your own ability. She wasn't comfortable with Callum knowing she could commune with Helios.

"If you do manage to conjure an artifact," said Callum, "Please let me see it as soon as possible. I am sure the other channeling masters will be impressed."

3

Anise awoke on a soft surface and sat up. She was on a cushioned couch in a glorious room. The sun was shining in through stained glass windows. She felt the presence of her circle of light, her little bubble of safety in the realm of dream. Though, if she hadn't, she might have thought that she was in the prince regent's room in the King's Seat in the city of Capitol.

Helios stood beside the couch, smiling indulgently down at her.

"Welcome to my home," he said. "You've dreamed yourself to me, this time."

Anise looked around some more. The place was worthy of being the home of a god. The fabric on the couch she had been lying on was cloth-of-gold. Everything was marble and stained glass.

An archway behind Helios led to a balcony above a courtyard. Below the balcony, standing in the yard, Anise could see a parked chariot. Beyond that was a field with horses running about. They looked a most unusual color. A bright orange or yellow, like they were made of flame.

Anise wondered if what she was seeing was from her imagination, her dream, or really from the dwelling place of Helios.

An elegant lady stepped into view. Her bearing felt as strong and proud to Anise as Helios', but she glowed with an inner calm where he radiated youth, energy, and intensity. There was a bright light coming from Helios and his crown, but this lady cast the soft glow of a full moon in her elegant flowing gown.

Helios swept his arm in front of the lady in a gesture of

introduction. "I believe you know my sister, Selene," he said.

"Mistress Luna," said Anise. Shyly she stepped closer to the woman, who enfolded her in an embrace. Anise felt a calm comfort flowing from the woman's arms.

"Anise," said Luna, "It's been a while."

4

A nise looked for the siblings' gift from the morning of the next day, even though Luna had said to look at twilight. "Look for a moment when the moon and sun are simultaneously in the sky."

She felt the warming presence of Helios on her shoulders when she walked to class in the morning, but Luna's company was mainly of the night.

After the evening meal, as Anise left the table to head back to the dorm room, her eye was caught by a glint of light. Something was shining in the afternoon sun on one of the windowsills of the common room.

Glancing around to make sure no one was watching her, Anise moved over to the window sill to see what had captured her attention. The light of the setting sun was cascading in through the window. It cast a warm glow over the sill and the wooden floor below.

Anise felt another presence as she looked at the window. There was a crescent moon in the sky, and its cooler glow mixed with the fading blush of the sun's light.

What had drawn her eye was something on the sill. Like before, with Sunshine's amulet, it was a raised knot in the wood at first. Anise touched the edge with her finger and lifted. Again, as her finger caught on the knot's edge, the sunshine mixing with the moonlight flowing through the window formed a metal shape.

It was a medallion, formed from sunshine, twin to the one she had conjured for Sunny. Twin, that is, until she saw the backside. Where Sunny's medallion had the impression of the knot in the wood on the back, this one had a back seemingly made of silver. An image of Luna's calming face showed on the silvery metal.

Anise lifted the amulet. A chain followed. Smooth and link-less, it had a pattern of gold woven with silver. It wove itself from the light streaming through the window as she raised it.

She placed the amulet over her neck. It settled into place and immediately made her feel safe. If she was in the sight of the sun or the moon, she knew that Helios or Luna would warn her of dangers.

5

Master Huginn was quite interested in Anise's speculations about the clairvoyance mystery. "It's certainly true, Anise," she said, "that it does feel like a big coincidence." She looked down at the speaking podium in front of her. Anise approached her after class as the other students left.

"The fading of the dragons is another mystery, and, as you say, the timing is suspicious." She waved with her hand in the general direction of the town. "Here in Ashton, the town guard is called the dragon's watch. That's not a fanciful name. They did fight off dragon attacks.

"That said," the master continued, "I'm hard-pressed to see the connection. Sometimes a coincidence really is a coincidence."

Anise shook her head. "I feel it," she said. "There is a connection. Maybe this Drun Coeloc person talked to the dragons and learned something from them. Maybe he stopped them from attacking."

Master Huginn considered Anise. She shook her head as well. "One thing I do remember from my own studies. Zoology. Dragons don't speak. They were thought to have intelligence. A certain malevolent intelligence, but they didn't speak."

"Not at all?" said Anise. She remembered Flambé at the Carnival of Wonders and her feeling that she could reach Flambé with her mind.

"Well," said Master Huginn, "there are stories of an ability called dragon-speak. It was apparently something some Academy mages could do. I think it was a rare talent. I'm not even sure what discipline it falls under.

"You know what, Anise," concluded the master, "I'll do some research. I'll let you know if I find any connection or useful information."

6

When Anise told Master Callum she had finished her project, he called her into his office. The masters mostly had offices in the same building on campus. The building was a large hexagonal marble structure called the Well. No one was sure why it was called that; it just was.

Anise hadn't been to the Well very often. It made her feel a little nervous. Like she might meet someone, or something, scary in the halls. But she braved it to talk to Master Callum about her project.

Master Callum pointed to the amulet on her neck. "Is that it?" he said. "Can I see it?" He held out his hand.

Anise hesitated. It was a very reasonable request, but the thought of taking off the medallion and putting it in Master Callum's outstretched hand felt wrong.

"I'll need to show it to the other channeling masters," said Callum. "We'll need to see it to grade it. They were very impressed when I told them what you planned. Master Lorenzo, especially, was quite curious."

Anise slowly took the amulet off. She hadn't had it very long, but she already felt naked and unprotected without it. It wasn't Master Callum. She trusted him. It was the idea of removing the medallion and especially the thought of leaving the master's office without it on.

She had gotten a sense of how it worked. She, Jord, Raphael, and Cian had had a snowball fight one afternoon after classes. Though the sun was beginning to set, she had felt the delicate touch of Helios's attention. Someone let fly with a snowball from behind her at one point. Usually, she would have been hit and might have complained about the sneak attack. But instead, she felt alert to the presence of the flying snowball in a way she didn't fully understand. It was like she could see the flight, even though it was directly behind her. She dodged it and acquired a reputation for having eyes in the back of her head.

Anise dropped the amulet into Master Callum's outstretched hand with a shiver.

7

The graduation ceremony was held in the auditorium. The auditorium was called the Dragon's Gullet Auditorium by the students. However, its official name was "The William Smith Memorial Auditorium." No one called it that because it was boring.

William Smith had been one of the founding members of the Academy. But, the students called the auditorium the Dragon's Gullet because what he was known for was crafting the bridge over the Serpent's Gorge.

The students who graduated from the Academy specializing in the element of earth often went into construction. Using one's control of the element of earth to construct large rock and earthen structures was an ancient art. Some among the masters argued that it was a bit of a lost art. Certainly, you would find few among the modern mages who would be able to make structures like the bridge over the Serpent's gorge or the Dragon's Gullet Auditorium.

The Dragon's Gullet Auditorium (Or, if you prefer, The William Smith Memorial Auditorium) was a miracle of construction. The outside walls were seamless sheets of polished granite. They towered over the neighboring buildings. You entered through doors at the base, and climbed, again seamless, spiral stone stairs to the top of the outside wall. A sweeping succession of benches arched into the distance, curving around the auditorium. The structure's interior was designed to carry voices from the central stage to all the seats.

The auditorium was used for events where the entire student body needed to hear things. There weren't very many of those. Even when all the staff, faculty, and students were sitting in the auditorium, it wasn't nearly filled. William Smith had had ambitions for the Academy.

The only other time Anise had been in the Dragon's Gullet was when she had attended Niall's graduation.

The graduation ceremony for Anise, and her class, was short and sweet. The faculty stood on the boards and called each student's name. The student called, stood, and walked a long and lonely walk up the stairs and across the stage. Then the headmaster of their discipline presented them with their Academy ring, followed by a kiss on the cheek.

It was the first time Anise had been so close to Master Lorenzo in her time at the Academy. She had seen him from a distance but hadn't spoken to him. He gave her an inquiring glance as he handed her her ring and kissed her cheek. But, he didn't say anything more than the congratulations he was offering to each student.

DREAM

1

Anise woke once again into a state of dream. She recognized it immediately, though she was a little confused, as she hadn't tried to enter the dream realm. Her control over her dreams recently was such that she didn't enter channeling dreams unless she chose.

She was lying in her own bunk in the dorm room. As usual in her channeling dreams in the dorm, the bunkbeds other than her own were gone. The room was filled with flickering candlelight. Anise sat up and looked around. It was darker than usual. At first, she didn't see anyone else there, then she noticed a shadowy figure standing against the wall on the far side of the room.

"Lord Helios?" Anise called out. "Where's your crown? Why's it so dark?"

The figure stepped a little closer, not quite into the light. Anise still couldn't make out who it was.

"You're not Lord Helios," she said. "Who are you? What do you want?"

The figure took another step closer. A voice Anise didn't recognize sounded out; quietly, calmly.

"Hello, Anise," it said, "don't worry, I just want to talk."

"How are you in my dream?" said Anise. "Who are you?"

The figure took another step forward, moving at last into the flickering light of the candle flames. It was Master Lorenzo.

2

Master Lorenzo stepped fully into the light of the candles. He smiled. A warmhearted, charming smile, full of good cheer and friendliness. He had a broad handlebar mustache. He looked younger and more robust here in the dreaming realm than in the waking world. He had seemed old and frail at the graduation ceremony.

"Anise," he said, "I didn't mean to startle you." He stepped forward, grabbed her hand, and pressed it to his lips. Even in the dream, the hairs of his mustache tickled her hand.

He continued, "I just wanted to congratulate you again on your graduation. I am proud of all the students who graduate from the Academy and my own channeling department. But, you, you seem to be something special."

"Master Lorenzo," said Anise, a little hesitantly. "How are you here? In my dream? Is this my dream? Are you a dream-walker like Master Callum?"

"Like Master Callum?" said Lorenzo. He laughed. "I suppose I am something of a dream-walker. And, as to whether this is your dream or not, I guess you could say it's both of ours. We're sharing this dream between us."

"But I didn't try to dream tonight," said Anise.

"I just want to say again how proud of you I am," said the master. "Your final project. That's something the likes of which we haven't seen in the years I've been teaching here. It's really something special. You can feel the power glowing from it. In fact, I found it a little familiar."

"Thanks ..." said Anise. She opened her mouth to continue, but the master kept talking.

"You aren't going to stick to the story you told Master Callum, are you?" Lorenzo smiled again. His smile had the comfort of an old tale told around a crackling campfire.

"There's more to that object than just a sun spirit or a moon spirit. You're talking to someone higher up, aren't you?"

3

Master Lorenzo nodded thoughtfully. "It's you," he said quietly to himself. "It's always been you." He reached down to his chest and fidgeted absentmindedly with the jade heart-shaped medallion he wore.

"Master Lorenzo," said Anise, "Are you the Watcher?"

"The Watcher?" said Master Lorenzo. "Do you mean do I watch my students, especially the channelers, in dreams to make sure they stay out of trouble? Of course I do."

"But, I felt the Watcher," said Anise, "He was angry, scared. He was worried about something."

"Anise," said the master, "I assure you. I have only the best interests of the Academy, the students, and Liamec at heart." Distractedly he clutched the jade medallion as he said this as if *it* was his heart.

"That's what Master Callum said," said Anise.

"And right he was, too," said Lorenzo.

"That medallion," said Anise. "I recognize it. It was Sebastian's. It belonged to the Knight of Moon & Shadow."

"Of course," said the master. "I kept it." He smiled again, somewhat ruefully this time. "I'm sure your uncle thought I kept it as a sign of contentment or satisfaction with what it had done to me. When, in fact, I kept it to remember what I could overcome."

Anise frowned.

"You know what time it is? In the waking world, I mean," said Lorenzo.

"Not really," said Anise.

"It's after the sun has set and before the moon has risen," said the master. It seemed like he came to a determination. He held out his hand toward Anise. "Come with me," he said, "I want to show you something."

4

Anise took Master Lorenzo's hand. He started to lead her toward the door of the dorm room. She hesitated and pulled back. "Master Callum says we should stay away from the edges of our circle of light."

Lorenzo laughed. "Master Callum doesn't know everything," he said. "You know the secret, don't you? The realm of dream is the same place where the clairvoyants go. They travel their paths of truth through this same realm. The truth is out there. There is something you need to see."

They reached the door, and the master pulled it open. At first, there was nothing but blackness outside. They stood side by side, looking out.

"Look closely, Anise," said the master, "Look closely; you'll see it."

Anise peered into the dark. After a bit, she did feel like she was starting to see something.

"You know," said Lorenzo, "Years ago, I tried to help a clairvoyant." He sounded angry. "I almost didn't know what a clairvoyant was. I tried to help her, and I failed." He had one hand in a firm grip on the wooden frame of the door and the other on Anise's shoulder.

"There were two things that I promised myself that I would do in her memory. First, I would bring back the study of clairvoyance so people like her could find help, and second, I would follow her teachings, her prophecies."

Anise shivered. The intensity in the master's voice was starting to scare her.

"Her prophecy told of a dark channeler. A powerful channeler. A channeler who would endanger the world, open the cracks of truth, and fracture the cosmos."

Master Lorenzo was almost yelling. His grip on Anise's

shoulder got tighter. "I'm the only one who knows what's wrong! I'm the only one who can fix it!"

"Master," said Anise, "You're scaring me."

Master Lorenzo grew noticeably calmer. "I'm sorry, Anise," he said. "I'm sorry for everything. There hasn't been a channeler as powerful as you born in two hundred years. You're the powerful channeler in the prophecy." His grip on her shoulder tightened. "As soon as I touched your medallion, I knew you were the one I had been looking for. You hid well, but that was your one mistake."

Anise tried to break free from his grip. "I haven't done anything," she yelled.

"But, you will," said Master Lorenzo. "Sometimes hard things have to be done for the good of everyone else." He shoved her in the back, directly toward the looming dark.

Anise teetered on the edge of the door frame. *It's only a dream*, she thought desperately. *I can wake up whenever I want.* She tumbled into the yawning blackness.

Anise's arms flailed as she fell. She opened her mouth to scream, but there was no air left for her lungs. The darkness of the dream swallowed her.

Dear Reader,

If you've reached this point and find yourself desperate to know what happens next, you've encountered the peril of middle books. They raise questions with great enthusiasm and then leave the answering to the final volume.

I hope *Death & Dragon* will bring you the answers you're hoping for—about Anise, her friends, her family, and what becomes of them all.

And if you enjoyed this book (cliffhanger and all), I'd be grateful if you left a quick review on Amazon. Your words help other readers discover the story—and help me keep telling them.

Thank you for reading,
J. Steven Lamperti

ACKNOWLEDGEMENT

Thanks to my beta readers: Claudia, John, Page, Mary, Harris, and Joerg.

Also, as always, to my alpha, Andrea.

BOOKS IN THIS SERIES

The Channeler Trilogy

Moon & Shadow

A young farmer.
An unexpected gift.
And powerful, deadly magic from the heavens...

One fateful evening in a quiet medieval village, Sebastian reaches up and pulls the moon down from the sky. As he sets off to market the next day, he discovers he can borrow mystical gifts from his fellow villagers: the delicate shadows of his true love's feet, the smelly wind of a dog's breath, the village fool's simplicity, and an arrogant man's brittle self-esteem.

When a terrifying monster attacks his village, the girl Anise, a survivor of the beast's assault on a neighboring town, helps Sebastian use the moon and his borrowed gifts as armor — turning the simple farm boy into the Knight of Moon & Shadow.

With Anise's help, Sebastian realizes it's up to him to protect his home from powerful enemies and safeguard the ones he loves. But on the treacherous path ahead, he must face the spirits of death, confront the shadows in his own soul, and navigate the enigmatic moon spirit, Luna.

If the Knight of Moon & Shadow can't destroy the source of the nightmare beasts, it'll be the end for his village and everyone he loves...

Moon & Shadow is the first book in J. Steven Lamperti's Channeler Trilogy. It's an enchanting YA Fantasy with sweet romance, quirky characters, and engaging humor. The unforgettable epic tale continues in Sun & Dream.

Death & Dragon

Trapped in the realm of dream and nightmare, will Anise wake up to save the land of Liamec from dragons and dream storms?

Anise has finished training in the magical arts at the Academy, the school where the wizards of Liamec learn to control their powers. But, one of the school's masters, the villainous Lorenzo, has banished her to the realm of dreams, trapping her there. When she finally wakes from her years of dreaming, the Kingdom of Liamec has changed.

Dragons are raiding the northern parts of the kingdom. Dream storms shake the fabric of the land. Anise is still being hunted by Lorenzo's nightmare beasts, twins to the ones her uncle fought in the village of Hero long ago. Can Anise stop the storms, brave the dangers, and save the kingdom?

In the sweeping conclusion to the award-winning Channeler Trilogy, J Steven Lamperti wraps up the threads spun in the earlier books.

Anise must return to the realm of dream, defeat Lorenzo, outmaneuver the dragons, and rescue Liamec from certain doom!

BOOKS BY THIS AUTHOR

The Wolf's Tooth

A lost baby boy.
A sun-dappled forest.
A pack of fierce wolves…

When a cheerful two-year-old discovers a group of sharp-clawed wolf cubs playing in a shady forest meadow, he befriends them without hesitation. When their mother cautiously accepts him into the den, Twee eventually becomes an accepted wolf pack member.

Torn from his lupine family by a devastating forest fire, Twee is thrust into the human world. From a prison cell to the clutches of an outlaw band, his journey is filled with hardship until he finds solace in Vix, a flame-haired street urchin who understands his longing for belonging.

A prophecy unveils a dangerous truth—the Young Lion, the kingdom's malevolent ruler, sees Twee as a threat. With an iron will and a sneer that curdles the soul, he will stop at nothing to keep Twee from unraveling his past.

As his outlaw friends face execution and the Young Lion relentlessly hunts him down, Twee fights for his life.

The Wolf's Tooth is the first book in J. Steven Lamperti's captivating Tales of Liamec series. Immerse yourself in this enchanting YA Fantasy, where action intertwines with poignant friendships, vibrant characters leap off the page, and a tapestry of mystery unfurls. The unforgettable series continues in By the Sea.

By The Sea

A young woman.
A perilous game of wits.
And a destiny that challenges the gods...

In the gray fishing village of Chelle by the Sea, Annabelle's life has been defined by the ebb and flow of the ocean and the weight of her brother's tragic demise. But when an enigmatic nobleman on a white horse arrives, everything changes.

Llyr, a stranger to both the villagers and Annabelle, brings a proposition that could alter her destiny. As they embark on an epic journey together, Annabelle must decipher Llyr's true intentions. Can she trust him with her life, or does he have his own hidden agenda?

In the spellbinding standalone second installment of the Tales of Liamec series, By the Sea, J. Steven Lamperti weaves a tapestry of magic, intrigue, and betrayal. Follow Annabelle and Llyr as they navigate treacherous waters, facing unimaginable obstacles and the wrath of the gods.

Discover a captivating tale of courage, friendship, and the ultimate test of wits. Join Annabelle and Llyr on their perilous quest that will challenge everything they believe in. Experience the enchanting world of Liamec in this unforgettable YA fantasy adventure.

Twilight's Fall

A young king, new to his realm.

His men slaughtered in a devastating ambush.
The kingdom's fate hangs on a sword's edge...

As trust shatters and betrayal lurks among his allies, Twilight, the young king of Liamec, must place his faith in the loyalty of those beside him. He and a few survivors embark on a treacherous journey back to the capital. His motley group of companions all rise to the occasion in ways he never expects. The young guardsman, Corentin, especially, has a mysterious secret power that may prove pivotal.

But safety eludes them, for the traitor has turned many of the land's nobles against their king. Reluctantly, Twilight must confront the looming prospect of a war against his own people, risking everything to save his kingdom, protect his queen Vix, and preserve his own life.

If the final battle arrives, will Corentin's mystical, hidden connection to the underworld hold the key to their salvation, or will this be Twilight's Fall, heralding the end of the kingdom of Liamec?

In J. Steven Lamperti's spellbinding tale of magic, treachery, and breathtaking battles, join King Twilight and his companions on an unmissable journey. Twilight's Fall is an epic YA fantasy novel that will sweep you into a world of thrilling adventure and pulse-pounding suspense. Grab your sword, stand alongside King Twilight, and prepare for an unforgettable battle that will shape the destiny of an entire kingdom.

Sunshine Over Hero

Strange things are happening in the village of Hero.

First it was the sheep—found drained of blood. Then village

girls began to disappear, returning days later with no memory of where they'd been.

Sunny, a sharp-minded farm girl with no patience for nonsense, is sure something unnatural is behind it. But when Raphael shows up—a traveling monster hunter whose last case was a mouse spirit stealing cheese—she realizes help might not be as heroic as she needs.

Raphael does have a few advantages: a talking silver sword named Cutter, a fire imp named Iggy who only ever says "Burn," and a willingness to follow Sunny's lead. The only problem? Cutter's eloquence and Iggy's enthusiasm don't always mix.

As the mystery deepens, the two uncover an ancient threat—and a connection neither expected.

Though part of the Tales of Liamec, Sunshine and Raphael's tale can be read alone—its own romp through fangs and fire.

Sunshine Over Hero is a romantic fantasy full of magic, mischief, and just a touch of bite—perfect for fans of Howl's Moving Castle and Legends & Lattes.

The Pirates Of Meara

A city built on stolen treasures.
Dark secrets and hidden truths.
Escaping Meara's cold-blooded pirates is their only hope...

Meara, a glistening pirate city adorned in turquoise and gold, holds deadly secrets. Mouse, a street-smart wharf rat with a mysterious power concealed behind a dirty eye patch, becomes an unlikely hero when he rescues Fern, the captivating daughter of a duke, from ruthless pirates. Together, they must navigate treacherous alleys, outsmart Bluebeard, the pirate lord pursuing them, and uncover enigmatic truths to reunite Fern with her father.

Time is running out, and the shadows of Meara grow darker. Betrayal lurks at every corner, testing their fragile trust as they fight for survival. They delve deeper, unearthing secrets buried beneath the city's streets and hiding under the vast expanse of the sea. Will Bluebeard catch Mouse and Fern before they can escape beneath the ocean's waves?

Embark on an unforgettable voyage with The Pirates of Meara, a thrilling standalone tale in J. Steven Lamperti's acclaimed Tales of Liamec fantasy series.

Endymion And The Fae

A shepherd boy, a girl of the fae, and a love that could heal—or divide—their worlds.

High in the mountain meadows, Endymion tends his sheep where mist clings to the slopes and old songs ride the wind. His life is simple—until he meets Lily, a girl of the Wee Folk with eyes like wildfire and a laugh like spring water.

To her people, she is Wee Folk. To his, she is Fae—a name spoken with fear, as if it carried danger of its own. What begins as a tender bond soon sets two worlds on edge.

When old wounds flare, Endymion must choose between peace and passion, tradition and hope. If he and Lily cannot bridge the divide, their love may cost more than their hearts.

A standalone tale within the Tales of Liamec, Endymion and the Fae is a gentle, slow-burn fantasy romance of first love, meadow magic, and quiet rebellion—for those who cherish cozy folklore, tender magic, and the stillness of high pastures.